MORTIMER AND ARABEL

Joan and Lizza Aiken
MORTIMER AND ARABEL

Illustrated by Quentin Blake

BBC BOOKS

Published by BBC Books,
a division of BBC Enterprises Limited,
Woodlands, 80 Wood Lane, London W12 0TT

First published 1992
© Joan Aiken Enterprises Ltd 1992
The moral right of the author has been asserted
ISBN 0 563 36396 7

Illustrations © Quentin Blake

Set in 13/16 pt Bembo Roman by
Phoenix Photosetting, Chatham, Kent
Printed and bound in Great Britain by
Redwood Press Ltd, Melksham

1

On a peaceful afternoon last year, Mr Jones
the taxi-driver was sitting on a bench in the
children's playground of Rumbury Town,
North London, reading an evening paper.
Arabel, his daughter, was swinging on one of
the swings. Mortimer, the family raven, was
walking along the top of the low fence that ran
round the play area, hunting for combs. Back at
home, in Number Six, Rainwater Crescent,
Mortimer had a collection of twenty-seven
combs already.

As he could not find any combs, Mortimer
whipped away an ice-cream cone from a two-
year-old child who was following him, and
swallowed it in one gulp, before the child could
let out a yell. Arabel did not see this. Nor did
the child's mother.

Mr Jones's alarm wristwatch played a short
tune, "Blow the Wind Southerly". Looking up
from the *Rumbury Evening Gazette*, he called,
"Arabel! Mortimer! Five minutes more! Then
we must go home."

"D'you want a swing before we go,
Mortimer?" said Arabel. She noticed that he had
stopped walking around the fence and was
staring hard at the ankles of a girl who was on
one of the swings.

"Krk!" said Mortimer thoughtfully.

Arabel lifted him on to a swing and began pushing him, which he greatly enjoyed.

"Come along, you two, that's enough now," said Mr Jones. "Knowing how slowly that blessed bird walks." He began to fold up his paper.

But Mortimer suddenly noticed the Wendy-house in a corner of the playground. It seemed to him a likely spot in which to find a comb. He flopped off the swing and dived through the doorway.

Two boys instantly shot out of the window, shrieking, with Mortimer close behind them. He had one boy's scarf wrapped round his beak. Then – dropping the scarf, which Arabel rescued and returned to its owner – he jumped on board the roundabout, dislodging several riders.

"*Mortimer!*" called Arabel. "We have to go home *now!*"

"Mortimer," said Mr Jones, "you'll get no black-treacle pudding ever again if you don't come along this minute."

But Mortimer continued to whirl joyfully round on the roundabout.

"Oh, look, Mortimer!" exclaimed Arabel cunningly, "I can see something pink lying on the ground outside the gate. Do you think it might be a comb?"

At once, Mortimer hurled himself off the roundabout and staggered dizzily towards the gate, scattering several small pocket combs from under his wings.

Arabel followed him, picking them up and putting them in her pockets.

"That bird needs a handbag," said Mr Jones.

"Kaaaark?" said Mortimer, interested.

"If he *has* to pick up articles from the gutter – which, mind you, is a *disgusting* habit –"

"Combs, Pa. He only picks up combs."

Mortimer picked up the pink comb. It was rather dirty.

"He only picks up combs *at the moment*. I can remember when it was wasps."

Mortimer blew a droning note on the comb, and then balanced it on his head. It fell off.

"Shall I make you a pocket, Mortimer?" said Arabel, helping him tuck the comb under his wing.

"Kaaak!" said Mortimer agreeably, and he began to walk towards home.

At this time, back in Rainwater Crescent, Mr Jones's three neighbours were busy working in their small front gardens.

Mr Coughtrack was trimming a leafy kangaroo, which he had cut, carved and snipped from a large box-bush. Its head touched one side-fence, and its tail the other. In fact, the tail had grown so long that it extended into the next garden, that of Mr Amstring, where there were knee-high models of Kings Cross, St Pancras and Victoria Stations, complete with trains.

As he stood up, after rearranging the Kings Cross destination board, the kangaroo's tail brushed Mr Amstring's face.

"Ahem!" he said loudly. "I don't wish to appear un-neighbourly, Mr Coughtrack, but if six inches aren't lopped off that beast's tail –

9

immediately – I shall be obliged to contact the Rumbury Borough Council cleansing department."

Mr Amstring was a short, skinny, nervous man, wearing green overalls and gloves. He looked, and sounded, very cross.

"Ahem! Mr Coughtrack!"

Mr Coughtrack was a large, hot, bald man. He stood up suddenly, snapping a large pair of shears, which made Mr Amstring start back.

"Eh?" he said. "Beg pardon? Did you speak, Mr Amstring?"

"I *said*, I would be obliged if you would take six inches off your kangaroo's tail."

"Off his *tail*?" said Mr Coughtrack, stunned.

At this moment Mr Jones, Arabel and Mortimer came along the street.

"Afternoon, Mr Coughtrack; afternoon, Mr Amstring," said Mr Jones, pausing to look over the low fence. "Show me up proper, your gardens do! I dunno how it is – time I've cleaned the old cab – and driven a few fares – and taken Arabel and the bird for a walk –"

Mr Amstring and Mr Coughtrack stopped glaring at each other and both looked with great disapproval at Mortimer, who had found a plastic cup in the gutter, and was jumping on it to flatten it.

"That really is a fine piece of work, that kangaroo of yours, Mr Coughtrack," Mr Jones said admiringly.

10

Mortimer's attention suddenly fixed on the bush-kangaroo. He flapped up on to the fence.

"*Get* that bird away from my topiary!" growled Mr Coughtrack, snapping his shears. "One step closer – and I'll clip his wings! It'll be rook pie –"

"Now, now, Mr Coughtrack! There's no need to take that tone. Mortimer was only admiring it," said Mr Jones.

"Mortimer is a raven, Mr Coughtrack, not a rook," said Arabel politely. But she lifted Mortimer off the fence. Luckily at that moment he saw something lovely in a drain grating, and forgot about the kangaroo.

Mr Amstring said threateningly, "If that bird of yours, Mr Joncs, so much as *breathes* on my stations – I shall have him removed by the Animal Warden."

"Oh, Mortimer isn't interested in stations," said Mr Jones hastily. "At least, not at present . . ."

Mortimer was now fishing another comb, a brown one, out of the grating. It was very dirty indeed. Arabel had to wipe it with a tissue.

"Pa's right," she told Mortimer. "You definitely need a pocket. I'll make you one the minute we get home . . ."

Followed by the hostile stares of Mr Amstring and Mr Coughtrack, they moved slowly along the pavement towards Number Six, Rainwater Crescent. Now they were passing the garden of

11

their neighbour Mr Leggit. It was full of huge sunflowers, big as satellite dishes. Among them, in a deckchair, sat their owner, keeping guard over his flowers with a water pistol.

"Good heavens!" said Mr Jones, startled. "Not expecting trouble, are you, Mr Leggit?"

Mr Leggit laughed sourly. He was old and skinny and stooped, with leather patches on his sweater elbows, and silver-rimmed glasses.

"*Trouble?*" he said. "Two years next door to that feathered fiend and not expect *trouble?*"

Faintly in the distance they heard the sound of a police siren.

"Been with you all day your bird – has he?" Mr Leggit asked in a meaningful tone.

"Why?"

"Big robbery up at the Town Hall. I heard they pinched the Mayor's pools winnings."

"Oh yes, I read about that in the *Evening Gazette*. But," said Mr Jones, relieved, "Mortimer's been with us all afternoon – good as gold – so it's all right, there's no –"

He glanced at Mortimer, who was thoughtfully moving towards a parked motorbike, studying its tyres while he whetted his beak on the pavement.

"Come on, Mortimer," said Arabel quickly. "As soon as we get home we can choose the stuff for your pocket."

The bike's owner jumped on it and rode off. Mortimer gazed after him sadly.

"All right?" said Mr Amstring. "All the Council wages stolen and you say it's *all right*?"

"They say," put in Mr Leggit, "that the thieves knew the combination to get into the safe-deposit room. They say it's that gang again – the lot they call the Cash and Carry Boys – who done the record shop in the High Street last summer –"

Mr Jones's watch began to play "Twinkle Twinkle Little Star".

"Oh, blimey," he said, "it's time for my fare, and your Ma told me to get some frozen spinach. Come on, you two!"

He hurried his daughter and raven along the street.

Mr Leggit watched after the Jones family as they went on their way and shook his head.

"Mind you," he said to the other two neighbours, "if Mr Jones hadn't said otherwise, I'd be fairly sure that bird had a hand in the affair –"

"A claw, it'd have to be, Mr Leggit," pointed out Mr Amstring morosely. "But I'm of your way of thinking."

"Arr!" agreed Mr Coughtrack. "Any trouble about the neighbourhood – you can be sure that bird's at the bottom of it . . ."

2

At Number Six, Rainwater Crescent, five minutes later, Mr Jones had left to drive a fare to a football match. Mrs Jones was busy making quince jelly and finishing off a black-and-white check jacket for Arabel. The jelly bubbled in a large pan on the stove, and a row of jampots stood ready to receive it when it was done. In the next room, Mrs Jones had fitted the jacket on to Arabel, and was turning up the sleeves, when they heard a crash from the kitchen.

"Mercy, what's that bird up to?" said Mrs Jones.

Mortimer had come in through his raven-flap, climbed up on to the ironing-board, from there to the work-top, and knocked a jampot on the floor. He had also dropped a few combs into the boiling jelly.

Arabel hastily pulled off the new jacket and ran into the kitchen.

"Mind Ma's quince jelly, Mortimer! It's very hot! I think you'd better come down from there."

She fished the combs out of the pan, and put Mortimer back on the ironing-board, where there were several snails.

"Can't leave that bird *five minutes*," mumbled Mrs Jones, coming in, her mouth full of pins.

"Take him in the other room, Arabel, lovey.
With his snails." And, as Arabel did so, she
called, "But don't let him near my knitting!"

The other room was piled high with
hand-sewn and knitted objects such as scarves,
sweaters and tea-cosies.

"There's some left-over bits of the black-and-
white stuff, Mortimer," said Arabel. "That one
would be big enough to make you a pocket.
We'll have to fold it like this, see, and cut it like
this –"

Using Mrs Jones's pinking scissors, Arabel cut
the doubled piece of cloth into a half-circle.
Mortimer watched with tremendous interest.

"Now," Arabel told him, "it has to be sewed.
Ma!" she called through the door. "Can I use the
sewing-machine?"

"Yes," called Mrs Jones, "if you're careful."

Arabel carefully removed the pinking scissors

from Mortimer (luckily he had not worked out how to use them) and put them on the mantelpiece. As she did so, Mortimer swallowed the reel of black cotton on the sewing-machine.

"Where's the black thread, Ma?" called Arabel.

"On the machine."

"No, it isn't."

"I suppose that bird's swallowed it?"

Mortimer looked as if his thoughts were far away.

"Oh well," called Mrs Jones, "there's another reel in the Jubilee tin."

Arabel put the new reel on the machine, threaded it, and began to sew.

Meanwhile, at the Town Hall, the Mayor, Mr Saddlejoy, was in despair. And so was his secretary, Doreen. Police were everywhere, and the whole place was a mess.

The phone on Doreen's desk rang, and she answered it distractedly.

"Oh, hallo, Mrs Saddlejoy!"

The Mayor scowled, and made head-shaking gestures.

"No, I'm afraid His Worship's with the police just now," said Doreen. "Yes, yes, the thieves took *everything*, yes, the knitting routines too, yes, they were all on the computer tapes, you know, as well as the one for operating the safe-

deposit room door. Yes, I'm ever so sorry, I'm
afraid they were the only ones. You could try
one of the other ladies, Mrs Saddlejoy, for the
patterns, Mrs Jones does ever such a lot, maybe
she'd be able to help you. I'm afraid I must get
off the line now, yes, it's dreadful, yes, I'm ever
so sorry, Mrs Saddlejoy –"

Doreen hung up.

"What's Lily on about *now*?" said the Mayor
gloomily.

18

"She wants a knitting pattern for a Fair Isle sweater. I told her to try Mrs Jones –"

"Sweaters!" said Mr Saddlejoy in disgust.

"For the Earthquake Relief, remember?" Doreen told him. "All the Townswomen's Guild ladies are knitting for Island Aid, the island of Polyandros, you know, there's only four days left before the Award Ceremony –"

"That's all I need, an Award Ceremony!" cried Mr Saddlejoy, tearing his hair. "And what am I to award? I presume all the prize tickets for the Island Cruise were in the safe-deposit room? As well as everything else?"

"Yes," said Doreen sadly.

At Number Six, Rainwater Crescent, the telephone rang. The phone in the Jones's house was halfway up the stairs, on the windowsill. Mortimer – now wearing his new pocket on his head – raced to the phone, kicked off the pocket, clasped the receiver with his claw, and was just about to yell "NEVERMORE!" into it, when Arabel gently removed the phone from him.

"Hallo?" she said. "This is the Jones house. Oh, hallo, Mrs Saddlejoy, shall I fetch Ma? No – no – that was our raven, Mortimer."

As she was saying this, Mortimer fell down four stairs, knocking over the umbrella-stand, which rolled in front of Mrs Jones as she came hurrying from the kitchen.

"Here she is now, Mrs Saddlejoy," said Arabel into the phone. "Ma, I mean. No, Mortimer is a he. It's Mrs Saddlejoy, Ma."

"Oh, hallo, is that you, Lil?" said Mrs Jones, pushing an umbrella off her foot. "Yes, I heard about the Town Hall burglary – *what*? You had the knitting patterns put on tapes? But that's terrible, I mean, whatever shall we do? Oh my stars, I'll be a broken rushlight without a pattern, I can only do scarves and tea-cosies – Yes, but, Lil, how *many* tea-cosies can they use in Poppyandry? Very well – whatever you say – maybe Mrs Amstring can help – 'Bye-bye."

She replaced the receiver, muttering, "What a thing, what can the thieves want with all those knitting patterns – I was going to do Fair Isle waistcoats in traditional hues –"

"What happened to them?" asked Arabel, puzzled.

"Abducted!" said Mrs Jones. "Every last one of them. They were at the Town Hall!"

A crash came from the kitchen.

"Oh, that bird!" screeched Mrs Jones. "I shall go deleterious one of these days!"

In the kitchen they found Mortimer, who was stirring the quince jam with a Chinese back-scratcher taken from the umbrella-stand. He had switched on the radio and dropped another jampot on the floor.

"*Rumbury Townswomen's Guild have asked us to remind you,*" said the radio, "*that there are very few*

20

days left before our special cruise ship sets off for Polyandros, Rumbury's twin town in the Southern Seas, with all your wonderful woollies on board. So: get your needles clacking for Island Aid! And don't forget, this year's star prize in the Rumbury Garden Gala will be tickets for the cruise. If your garden catches the judge's eye as he tours the streets, your family could be our Official Aid Ambassadors on a wonderful, wonderful cruise to Polyandros!" And the announcer finished by bursting into song: *"Knit a little bit! Knit a little bit for Island Aid!"*

In the middle of this, Mr Jones came in, and hung his cap on the hook at the back of the kitchen door.

"Garden Gala," he muttered. "So that's what all the neighbours are up to." He glanced at the broken glass on the floor. "Any chance of a cup of tea?"

"Oo, Ben, I'm ever so sorry!" cried his wife. "I was on the phone to Lil, didn't notice the time. It'll be ready in two shakes – it was all that about the knitting patterns at the Town Hall –"

She popped a pizza and two sausages into the microwave.

Mr Jones looked bewildered. "Knitting patterns at the Town Hall?"

"You know, Ben, me and the ladies are all knitting for the victims of Polly-ade, sweaters and tea-cosies it was to have been, well now it'll just be the cosies –"

"I thought it was hot down there, tropical?"

21

said Mr Jones. "What do they want with tea-cosies?"

"Well, for the shock, I suppose, after the earthquake, they do say hot, sweet tea –"

One of Mrs Jones's completed tea-cosies was moving along the floor. Mrs Jones shrieked and dropped an egg. Arabel picked up the cosy and found Mortimer underneath.

"*That*'s not your pocket, Mortimer," she said. "Look, I put your pocket up here. I found it on the stairs."

She handed Mortimer his black-and-white pocket.

"All the knitting patterns have been hijacked from the computer at the Town Hall," Mrs Jones told her husband, putting on a new egg to boil.

"Why?" he said, baffled.

"The thieves took them, Pa," explained

Arabel. "Along with the Council wages, and tapes, and the plan for the new motorway that's to go through the comprehensive school and the swimming baths –"

"Really?" said Mr Jones, interested. "That'll be a handy way from the station to the shopping mall."

His wife put down a plate of pizza and sausages in front of him.

"Come on, Mortimer," said Arabel. "I'll sew some strings on your pocket."

Meanwhile, at the Town Hall, Mr Saddlejoy was talking to the police.

"Somewhere in the passage outside this room," he told Sergeant Cutlink, "there is a concealed door: the door to the safe-deposit room. It will only open in response to an electronic message."

"And what is this message, Your Worship?" asked Sergeant Cutlink, scribbling in his notebook.

"It's a song. It has to be sung four inches from the concealed electronic button –"

"Where is the button?"

Doreen said: "The chart showing the whereabouts of the button is on a computer program, but the tapes –"

"Don't tell me, they've all been stolen," said the Sergeant. "And what is the song?"

"If we knew *that* –" snapped the Mayor.

Doreen explained: "The songs are programmed to change every day – there are three hundred and sixty-five of them. They have all been recorded, and indexed with a list of the dates when they are played. But that's on –"

"One of the stolen tapes," finished Sergeant Cutlink. He muttered to himself, "Cor, stone my aunt Mabel!"

At the Jones house, Arabel had sewed the
strings on to Mortimer's pocket, put some of his
combs inside it, and hung it round his neck. He
hopped to the floor, and several combs fell out.
Picking them up, Arabel noticed a sheet of paper
with a message on it in her mother's printing.
She called:

"What's P.O.R. mean, Ma?"

She took the piece of paper through to the
kitchen, where her father was starting to eat
his tea.

"P.O.R.?" said Mrs Jones, puzzled. "Prisoner
on Run? Plate of Radishes? – Oh, I know, Put
out Rubbish. They've changed the day, because
Bank Holiday fell on National Yoghurt Day."

"I'll do the rubbish for you, Martha," said Mr
Jones, putting down his fork. "Got a sack?"

"Finish your tea first, dear,
I'll write it on the board,"
said his wife, and she wrote
P.O.R. on the chalkboard
she kept above the stove.

Mortimer came proudly
in, wearing his pocket
with a fan of combs
in it like a feathered
head-dress.

"Ju-seppi Verdi!" gasped
Mr Jones. "What's that?"

"It's Mortimer's pocket,"
said Arabel.

25

"Thought he'd joined the Druids."

"Mind you, don't put anything in it *but* combs, Mortimer, my boy!" said Mrs Jones. "*Oo, Ben!* What are those cassettes on the table? They aren't Lily's knitting tapes?"

"You've got knitting tapes on the brain, Martha," said her husband. "No, those cassettes are a stroke of genius I had. You know this *Music While You Ride* they have –"

"Stupid, I call it! Who wants to hear all that reggae-gurgitation between Oxford Circus and Tufnell Park?" demanded Mrs Jones.

"Ah, my tape's not that sort," said Mr Jones. He sliced the top off his boiled egg, not observing that Mortimer was climbing up the back of his chair, and went on, "*My* music is to remind people that they're better off riding in a cab than trying to squeeze into a rush–hour train –"

At this moment Mortimer dived head–first into Mr Jones's egg, which fell to the floor.

"*I* don't know why everyone in this house isn't a Histrionic Paragon!" screamed Mrs Jones, running for a mop, which she shook at Mortimer. "*Look* what you've done, you umbrageous bird! Get out of my sight! Go and sit in the coal–hole!"

"Oh, Mortimer," said Arabel. "You *have* made a mess of your pocket!"

The pocket was now covered in boiled egg, sausage grease, and pizza sauce.

"Kaaark," said Mortimer peevishly.

"Ma," said Arabel, "can we wash Mortimer's pocket?"

Without speaking, Mrs Jones seized the barbecue tongs, whipped the pocket away from Mortimer, and dropped it into the washing machine. Then she said, "That bird doesn't *deserve* a pocket."

"Oh, come on, Martha. You can't expect him to behave like a human –"

"Human? He behaves like a Tyrannosaurus Reckless!" said Mrs Jones, sweeping up boiled egg and broken china.

Mortimer sulkily climbed under the laundry basket, which had fallen over.

Giving up on his tea, Mr Jones went into the lounge and switched on the TV, which said, *"Police believe that the Cash and Carry Boys, known to have committed several recent burglaries, may be connected with today's theft of securities and computer tapes from the Town Hall. Two men in their mid-twenties were seen driving the getaway vehicle, now found abandoned in Rumbury Park . . ."*

Arabel, who had listened to the News for a minute, went back into the kitchen.

"Shall I read you a story about dinosaurs, Mortimer?" she said, lifting up the laundry basket.

But Mortimer was no longer under the basket.

3

"Where's my tapes, Martha?" said Mr Jones, coming into the kitchen. "They were on the table just now."

"Mercy!" said Mrs Jones. "They've been stolen! By the Town Hall tape thieves! Tape collectomaniacs!"

"More likely that bird's had them. Where is he?"

"Yes – where *is* Mortimer?" said Mrs Jones.

"Well, you told him to go and sit in the coal-hole," said Arabel. "I think he was upset about his pocket."

"Upset! The day that bird shows any feeling I'll turn in my grandma's grave."

"He isn't in the coal-hole now," reported Mr Jones, coming back from outside. "– *Oh, my gawd!* I didn't put him out with the rubbish, did I?"

"No, it's not out yet," said Arabel. "Remember, you wrote P.O.R. on the slate."

"And what's this?" said Mrs Jones, looking at the slate. 'K.S.J.'?"

"Keep stirring jam, Ma," said Arabel.

"The jam! Oh, my heavens!" Mrs Jones rushed to the pan of simmering jam. "You don't think that Mortimer – and the tapes – you don't *think* – ?"

At this time, in a passage of the Town Hall
building, two policemen were singing. One,
standing on a chair, sang "Humpty Dumpty Sat
on the Wall". One, lying on the floor, sang,
"Oh, Dear, What Can the Matter Be".

In the Mayor's office, Sergeant Cutlink was saying to Mr Saddlejoy:

"The men will be working in shifts, sir. We are expecting to cover every square metre of the wall and sing three hundred and sixty-five songs a day. That way I calculate we have an eighty-six per cent chance of finding the concealed electronic button before the end of the year . . ."

At the Jones house, Arabel's father called her.

"Better come in out of the garden, lovey. Mortimer will turn up, don't you fret. He's probably after Mrs Coughtrack's Ginger."

As Arabel came slowly through the back door, Mr Jones's watch played "Lilliburlero".

"Here," he said. "I've got to dash again. Why don't you make your Ma a nice cup of coffee? She'll wear herself to ribbons, knitting, the way she's going. You do that, lovey, 'Bye, both of you, see you later."

"Yes, I'd *love* a cuppa," said Mrs Jones, knitting away. "I daren't stop, or I'll lose my place – two, four, six, eight –"

When Arabel pressed the switch of the coffee machine, two cassettes suddenly shot out of the toaster.

"There! What did I tell you?" said Mrs Jones. "You can't put a *thing* down in this house without him laying his claws on it –"

With a loud clang the washer door burst open,

and Mortimer tumbled out of it, warm, sleepy, and rumpled, with his washed pocket (slightly shrunk and the colours run) around his neck.

"Oh, Mortimer!" said Arabel, delighted. "There's some spaghetti hoops left from my supper. Would you like them?"

"Kaaark!" said Mortimer.

"Always falls on his feet, that bird does," said Mrs Jones. "Waited on, beak and claw."

Arabel gave Mrs Jones her coffee and Mortimer his spaghetti.

"Pop a tape on the player, will you, pet? Some music to keep me going," said Mrs Jones, knitting away madly.

"I'll put on one of Pa's tapes," said Arabel.

After a moment or two there boomed out a tremendously loud voice from the speaker.

"*MIND – THE – GAP!*"

"Oooo!" shrieked Mrs Jones, dropping half a dozen stitches.

"Kaaark!" gasped Mortimer, falling backwards off the table with his bowl of spaghetti.

The tape continued with its announcement.

"Stand clear of the doors! *Mind* the gap! Stand *clear* of the doors! Passengers for High Barnet take the first train from this platform and change at Camden Town."

Then the tape played a noise of train doors closing, and the kind of conversation you hear on the Underground.

"Mind your umbrella! That's my ear! Excuse *me*, you are on my foot. *Do* you mind?"

Mrs Jones sprang up to switch off the cassette player, and skidded on Mortimer's spaghetti.

"*Look* at that bird's clean pocket! Covered in spaghetti already!" she scolded. "This time it goes in the bin. I'm not washing it again."

And she thrust the spaghetti-covered pocket into the rubbish bin under the sink.

Mortimer gave her a dreadful look.

In the Town Hall, Doreen was handing the
Mayor some Chinese takeaway when one of the
policemen, PC Barnoff, came in to let Mr
Saddlejoy know that he had to go off on local
duty.

"But they'll soon be sending a replacement,"
he whispered. "A baritone from the Police
Choir."

"Why are you whispering?" asked Mr
Saddlejoy, glancing round the room for unseen
listeners.

"A bit hoarse, sir," whispered PC Barnoff.
"Singing non-stop for seven hours."

"You'd better pop by a late-night chemist for
a bottle of gargle," Doreen told him
sympathetically.

Up at Rumbury playground it was pitch dark.
Two men, members of the ill-famed Cash and
Carry Boys, were lurking beside the phonebox.
They wore stocking masks. Their names were
Bill and Joe. A car drove slowly by, and they
ducked out of sight. Then the bell in the
phonebox rang. Joe dashed for the door, opened
it, and grabbed the receiver.

"Eh?" he said. "Oh. – Thanks a *bunch!* We
only waited half an hour! *Why* can't you come?"

"Trouble with neighbours in the Crescent,"
rasped the voice from the phone.

A taxi pulled up in the road outside.

"Yeah, yeah," said Joe on the phone. "We'll stash them somewhere safe – 'bye-bye, Leggy –"

"That's *enough!*" hissed Bill. "There's someone *outside.*"

The Cash and Carry Boys pulled off their stocking masks and beamed affably at the person outside, who happened to be Mr Jones.

While Mr Jones entered the phonebox, and started trying to put coins in the slot, Bill and Joe wandered away into the playground and casually buried something in the sandpit.

Back in Rainwater Crescent, Arabel had just finished making Mortimer a second pocket, and Mrs Jones, for a change, was crocheting a tea-cosy, when the front doorbell rang.

Mortimer dashed for the door, knocking a tin full of pins on to the floor.

"Oo, mercy," said Mrs Jones. "That'll be Mrs Whatsit with the Prussian blue wool. Get the door, will you, Arabel dearie, while I just count these stitches –"

But when Arabel, carrying Mortimer's new pocket, opened the front door, she found a policeman outside.

"What is it, please?" asked Arabel.

She was puzzled when the policeman addressed her in a whisper.

"Is this the house of Mr Ben Jones?"

"Yes, it is," whispered Arabel politely in reply.

Now Mrs Jones came into the hall, carrying her basket of crochet.

"It's about your husband, Mrs Jones," whispered PC Barnoff.

Mrs Jones dropped the basket.

"Oh! Ben!" she wailed. "Where *is* he? What's *happened*? I *knew* it would happen some time – he's been mugged by armed Kamikazes – I always said he should get one of those milkmen's computerized lock safes in his cab –"

She seized Mortimer's pocket from Arabel and mopped her face with it. Then Mortimer, who had been watching her, took the chance to remove the pocket from her hand.

"We're looking for your husband," whispered PC Barnoff.

"He's been *kidpanned!*" said Mrs Jones. "Have they sent a lock of his hair? – his watch? – *anything?*"

Mortimer thoughtfully swallowed his new pocket.

4

In the kitchen at Number Six, Rainwater
Crescent a few minutes had passed. PC Barnoff
was fanning Mrs Jones with a copy of the
Rumbury Evening Gazette. Mrs Jones was on a
chair, with her eyes shut, moaning weakly.
Arabel was collecting a mass of pins from the

floor with a giant magnet, and putting them back in the pin tin.

Mortimer was trying to open the cupboard under the sink. He had suddenly remembered that Mrs Jones had put his first pocket there, in the sink bin.

But he could not reach the catch of the cupboard door.

Opening her eyes, Mrs Jones glared at the policeman, and demanded, "Who are *you*? And where's Ben?"

"I'm PC Barnoff, Mrs Jones," he whispered. "Come to ask Mr Jones some questions –"

Mrs Jones shut her eyes again.

"Why do we have to whisper?" whispered Arabel.

PC Barnoff pulled a bottle of gargle from his pocket and gargled with it.

"That's better," he croaked. "A bit hoarse – singing all day at the Town Hall –"

And, to Mrs Jones, he said, "We'll soon have you right, Missus. How about a cup of tea?"

He sponged Mrs Jones's brow with a sponge handed him by Arabel, who put on the kettle and went to get a tea-bag.

Mortimer was now sitting on the edge of the sink, reaching down, trying to open the cupboard below him. His tail feathers had started to singe in the gas flame under the simmering jam saucepan.

"Is something burning?" croaked PC Barnoff.

"Oh, Mortimer!" said Arabel. "Your tail!"

"Kaaark!" said Mortimer, much impressed by the blue smoke. He jumped into the sink, which was full of water and dishes. Some water slopped on the floor.

"I can smell burnt feathers!" moaned Mrs Jones. "Has somebody fainted?"

The kettle began to whistle.

Mrs Jones stared at PC Barnoff and remembered. "Ben's been abnegated! Tell me *quick* – is he dead?"

Holding the boiling kettle, PC Barnoff said. "All I wanted was help with inquiries."

"You mean," gasped Mrs Jones, "Ben's *murdered* somebody?"

Out in the hall the telephone rang.

Arabel ran to answer it. "Rumbury 3482," she said. "Yes – it is. I beg your pardon? I'll have to ask –"

Running back into the kitchen, she said, "A lady asks, will we accept a reverse charge call from a Mr Jones."

"Aaaaah!" screamed her mother. "They've got Ben incorporated! Let me speak to him – if it's for the last time –"

She tottered towards the hall.

"Just a minute, ma'am!" exclaimed PC Barnoff, hurrying after her. "Before you speak on that line – I'll attach an appliance to the instrument –"

As he spoke, he was trying to open his

briefcase, which could only be undone by means of an electronic whistle.

"Instrument?" said Mrs Jones, puzzled. "You mean the piano?"

Mortimer came into the hall, dragging the kitchen magnet.

"Now you can speak, ma'am," said PC Barnoff, who had attached some wires to the telephone. "I'll be able to trace the call in seven minutes."

"Wh – what shall I say?" faltered Mrs Jones.

"Just whatever you *would* say – under the circumstances –"

Mortimer, still holding the magnet, was taking a lot of interest in the whistle which hung from PC Barnoff's belt.

"Ben?" whispered Mrs Jones. "Is that you? Have they got you tied up? Drugged? Starved?"

"Starved?" said Mr Jones in the playground callbox. "I've only been gone an hour. I was going to ask if I should bring some Chinese takeaway –"

"*Chinese?*" gulped Mrs Jones. "Have they cut any bits off you? Fingers? *Ears?*"

"Look, Martha," he said. "I'm in the phonebox; not the operating theatre."

"You haven't been kidnapped?"

Arabel told the policeman, "I *think* my raven's going to eat your whistle, Mr Barnoff."

There was a short, sharp struggle.

"Martha? Martha?" shouted Mr Jones in the

callbox. "What's going *on* there? Have you had a break-in?"

But all that he could hear, coming from the phone, was an ear-splitting whistle.

Baffled, Mr Jones hung up and left the box. Outside it, he found Bill and Joe, leaning against a wall.

"You two still here?" he said. "Bit old for the playground, aren't you?"

"Looking for old Leggy's tortoise," replied Joe. "Lifelong pal. Had him seventeen years. Amnesic with grief."

Mystified, Mr Jones got into his taxi and drove off.

Back at Rainwater Crescent, PC Barnoff was saying: "That call came from the phonebox by the children's playground, Mrs Jones."

Things were calmer in the Jones house now. They were drinking tea in the kitchen. The policeman's fingers were bandaged.

"*I* could have told *you* that," said Mrs Jones. "That's where he always phones from. But why do you want him to help you?"

"He drives about such a lot, he might easily have seen something suspicious –"

Mortimer was sulking and frustrated. He had been given a biscuit, but he was standing on it, not eating it.

"I'm *sorry* your pocket got put in the rubbish bin, Mortimer," Arabel whispered to him. "What happened to the other one I made you?"

Mortimer did not answer.

"I'll make you another one, I promise."

"No more sewing tonight," said her mother. "That bird can wait till tomorrow."

"Thanks for the tea, Ma'am," said PC Barnoff. "If your husband should have any information for us, could he call this number –" He gave Mrs Jones a card.

"I'd better write it on the slate." Mrs Jones balanced the card on top of the board, and saw him to the door.

The moment after PC Barnoff had left, the phone rang again.

"*Now* who can it be?" said Mrs Jones nervously. "Don't you two talk to *anybody* while I'm speaking –"

She picked up the phone.

"Yes? Who is it? Oh, it's you, Lil. I was going to call you – but things have been happening here. Listen, Lil – when you get to the part where you have to cast off – knit two together, purl two – *then* what?

"It's in *Swedish*?

"Oh, you have a Swedish *au pair*?"

While she talked, Mrs Jones continued knitting, and her ball of blue wool rolled down the stairs.

Mortimer came out into the hall.

"Snodd maska?" said Mrs Jones. "And then there's a monster? Oh, a monster's a pattern stitch? A styng monster? Hoger sticka, vanster sticka – left needle, right needle –"

Mortimer quietly swallowed the ball of blue wool. Then he began to move up the stairs towards the other end of the wool, which was attached to Mrs Jones's knitting. She let out a shriek. The wool broke.

Mortimer hastily retired to the kitchen and went out through his raven-flap.

Luckily at this moment Mr Jones came home. He put out the rubbish in its black sack, and gave a comic to Arabel, who went upstairs to bed.

While he was eating his supper – in front of the lounge fire for comfort – Mrs Jones told her husband about PC Barnoff's visit.

"*Why* he told me you'd been abducted when you hadn't –" she said. "And then, Mortimer bit him – But he came here to warn you about that gang, the Cash and Carry Boys, the ones who stole all that stuff from the Town Hall –"

"But why ever should the cop come to our house?" said Mr Jones.

"Because the thieves went up this way, past the old railway roundhouse, where they used to have their hi–de–hi hole, so they went there –"

"Who went there?"

"The police went there. But they weren't there, so then they came here, in case they'd come here – they tracked with tracker dogs. But then – when I told them Mortimer had dragged his kipper along Rainwater Crescent –"

"What am *I* supposed to do?" said Mr Jones, rather baffled.

"He left a number. If you should see anything suspicious, do not enter into armed contact with the miscreants, but combat the number – it's on top of the kitchen board –"

"I'll note it down now," said Mr Jones, carrying his empty plate to the kitchen, and then he said, "Oh, blimey!"

"What's the matter?" called Mrs Jones from the other room.

Mortimer had, with some difficulty, dragged the black plastic sack of rubbish into the kitchen through his raven-flap. He had then dug into the sack and rummaged about until he found the first pocket Arabel had made him, all covered in tomato sauce. This he had wrapped comfortably

round his neck, and had then burrowed himself
a cosy nest among the orange peel, old yoghurt
pots, dead flowers and dirty paper.

"Nothing's the matter," called Mr Jones to his
wife.

"You and that mess can wait till the
morning," he told Mortimer.

"Kaaark," said Mortimer sleepily.

"Oh – Ben –" called Mrs Jones. "Could you
put the mousetrap by the veg rack? It's baited
with cheese ready – it's on the top –"

"Okay," called Mr Jones. After putting down
the trap, he took off his watch and hung it on a
hook by the sink.

"Goodnight, Mortimer. Mind the mousetrap,
now!"

Mr Jones left the kitchen, turning out the
light. The moment after he did so, a hand came
through the raven-flap.

5

Mortimer the raven, wearing his pocket which
was soaked in sauce, slept peacefully in the
Jones kitchen, comfortably snuggled down
among a lot of dirty papers and dead flowers.

But suddenly he woke up because he heard
something come through his raven-flap and a
hand shoot back the bolt of the door. The door
opened, and a dark figure crept into the kitchen,
moving very softly.

Mortimer, still wearing his pocket, climbed,
with great speed and equal silence, on to the
work-top and along to the toaster and cassette
player.

The intruder tiptoed across the room to the
grandfather clock. On his way he removed
Mr Jones's watch, which hung, glowing, on its
hook by the sink.

Mortimer, from the shadows by the toaster,
attentively watched the black figure. It seemed
to be carrying a sack. The door of the clock
creaked. The intruder seemed to be taking
objects from the sack, and putting them inside
the clock.

Mortimer pressed the button of the cassette
player, and a shatteringly loud, deep voice
announced in commanding tones:

"*MIND – THE – GAP!*"

The intruder let out a wail of utter shock and terror, leapt away from the clock, and set off the mousetrap, which clanged sharply and flung a piece of cheese across the kitchen.

Meanwhile the cassette was going on with its instructions: "Stand – *clear* – of – the – doors. *Mind* the gap. Stand *clear* of the doors."

Moaning with panic and confusion, the intruder bolted for the back door, knocking over a kitchen stool and tripping over various cans and jars, which Mortimer had removed from the garbage bag.

Mr Jones came down the stairs, wearing pyjamas and carrying a cricket bat.

"You stay up there, Martha, till I see if it's burglars," he ordered his wife, who was leaning over the stair-rail in her curlers.

"What's that rushing noise?" she wailed. "Is it a flood? Has Rumbury Reservoir burst its banks? – You stay right here, lovey," she told Arabel, who now came out, in her blue dressing gown, "in case the water rushes in. Oh, my tea-cosies!"

"Shut up, Martha," said her husband, going into the kitchen. "There's no flood. Mortimer's been playing with the cassette player, that's all "

Mrs Jones and Arabel came slowly down, and into the kitchen.

"Where *is* Mortimer? Oh, my gawd, *what's all that on the floor?*"

"Oh, that's nothing," said Mr Jones hastily. "Mortimer left it like that last night."

"And you never troubled to clear it up, well really!"

"That's funny," said Mr Jones, ignoring this. "The back door's open."

He shut the door and bolted it.

"I expect Mortimer fled with a guilty conscience," muttered Mrs Jones.

"No, he can't undo the bolt. Somebody *must* have been in."

Just then there came a ghostly tapping from the grandfather clock. Its door swung slowly open.

"They're hiding in the clock!" shrieked Mrs Jones. "*Do* something, Ben! Boiling oil –"

Mortimer emerged from the clock.

"Oh, Mortimer, you found your first pocket!" said Arabel warmly, lifting him down.

"You've been messing about with my tapes!" accused Mr Jones.

"Well, Pa, it did frighten away the burglars," Arabel pointed out.

"I should have listened to the constabulary," lamented Mrs Jones. "Oh, Ben! His card! We must combat him immediately."

"We don't know yet what they've taken," objected Mr Jones.

His wife was hunting for PC Barnoff's card, since the slate, which had fallen over, was covered with quince jam, and the numbers on it could not be read.

"Perhaps the card blew on to the floor while

the door was open," said Arabel, hunting as
well.

"The crown jewels could be on *this* floor and
even Mortimer couldn't find them," grumbled
Mrs Jones.

"I'll just call 999," said Mr Jones, making for the phone. His wife and daughter followed, to hear what he would say.

Mortimer, hungry after all the excitement, browsed among the rubbish by the back door, looking for a toast crust or an apple core.

A hand came through the raven-flap, holding Mr Jones's watch, which it swung from side to side. After watching this thoughtfully for a moment, Mortimer shot his head forward and swallowed the watch. The hand grabbed him round the neck, and dragged him through the flap. Mortimer, busy swallowing the watch, had no time to protest.

Then the back door opened again, and feet tiptoed across the kitchen . . .

"Well, I suppose I'd better put the kettle on," sighed Mrs Jones, when her husband had finished reporting the break-in. And she did so.

Just as the kettle began to whistle, the front doorbell rang, and Mr Jones let in PC Barnoff.

"So: what is it this time?" asked the policeman. He sounded tired.

"Marauders, Mr Barnet! Pillage and larceny and sockage! We've left circumstances exactly as we found them," explained Mrs Jones proudly, while PC Barnoff looked with some disapproval at the mess on the floor.

"We heard this noise," Mr Jones told him,

"and I came downstairs – and the back door was open."

"Like it is now?"

"Yes," said Mr Jones. And then he said, "That's odd; I thought I closed it."

"And the interlopers left all this mess on the floor?"

"Well no; I'm afraid that was our bird. – I believe you've met Mortimer?"

PC Barnoff looked at his bandaged fingers. He said:

"And where might *he* be? At this moment in time?"

"He was here just now. He scared off the intruders by playing a tape."

"Hmn," said PC Barnoff distrustfully. "It's a pity he's not available. So, what appears to be missing? Apart from your bird?"

"Maybe some of my scarves and cosies," worried Mrs Jones. "It's hard to tell. You see the list fell in the jam –"

Arabel suddenly said: "The cassette player's missing, Pa."

"No, it's not, dearie, it was playing its head off just now –" Then Mr Jones looked at the shelf. "That's *crazy*. It *has* gone. Did you move it, Martha?"

"Those gladiators must have been in here all the time!" wailed Mrs Jones. "And, while you were on the phone, they nipped out and abdicated with it –"

"But we were only out of the room a couple of minutes," said Mr Jones, feeling in his pocket, then glancing at the hook by the sink. "My watch – Hey! That's gone too! If that blasted bird has had it – Where *is* Mortimer, anyway?"

There was a loud crash outside the open back door, and Mortimer staggered in, swaying a bit, with a sock over his head.

"It's the hooded avenger, the rat-man!" shrieked Mrs Jones.

"No, it's Mortimer," said Arabel. "He must have been kidnapped."

She picked up Mortimer and removed the sock.

"Could *he* have removed the cassette player?" suggested PC Barnoff.

"Well – he did eat my Elizabeth Arden perfume atomizer that time," admitted Mrs

Jones. "But to say he'd eat a cassette player is just plain *silly*."

PC Barnoff suddenly felt he'd had enough. He snapped, "May I suggest that, until you can produce *any* definite evidence, you had best keep that bird under restraint; or I shall be forced to alert the proper authorities."

And he stomped out of the house.

Outside, in the street, two dark figures watched as the police van drove off.

Back in the kitchen, Mr Jones was saying, "You know, Martha, *I* don't think that fellow took us seriously; he didn't believe there'd been a burglar."

"*Course* there was a burglar," said Mrs Jones indignantly, tidying up. "Why shouldn't we be burgled? We're as good as them at the Town Hall."

"Were they trying to steal Mortimer?" asked Arabel anxiously.

"Nevermore!" said Mortimer in a doleful voice, looking down at where his pocket should be hanging, but was not.

Then, suddenly galvanized, he rushed into the other room.

"What's got into him?" said Mr Jones. "The workings of that bird's mind would puzzle Einstein."

A short time later, two dark figures were banging loudly on Mr Leggit's door.

"Whoever it is, go away!" said a voice from inside.

"But it's us, Mr Leggit!"

"The sunshine boys!"

Mr Leggit snatched open the door. He was wearing a dressing gown, and one sock.

"What the fiery fungus are you two doing here at this hour?" he hissed. "Go away! You shouldn't have come here."

"We came to keep you company," said Joe. He smelt of beer. He sang: "Singing tooral-aye-ooral-aye-oddity, Oh tooral-aye-ooral-aye-eh –"

Bill joined in. "If a man has no neighbours to nod at, he rapidly dwindles away."

"I shall call the police!" threatened Leggit. "If you don't clear off –"

"*Police*, he says," said Joe.

"Police. That's serious. All right, Grandpa –"

"We're on our way."

They hopped off, crashing through his sunflowers.

In the Joneses' kitchen, the mess had been mostly cleared off the floor, when Mortimer suddenly appeared in the doorway, shoving the sewing-machine ahead of him. It was heavy; but Mortimer was very, very strong.

"Arabel Jones! You are *not* to make another

54

pocket for that blessed creature till we've all had some sleep."

"But his other one's gone," said Arabel. "He was wearing it when he tried to catch the burglar. His pocket's been stolen!"

Meanwhile Mortimer had shoved the sewing-machine up against the grandfather clock, climbed on it, and opened the clock door. He climbed up and there was a crash as he disappeared headfirst inside.

"Oh, my stars!" cried Mrs Jones. "What's *in* there?"

Mortimer reappeared with a piece of railway-track in his beak.

Mr Jones rushed to the clock and looked inside.

"*Please* be careful!" warned his wife. "It could be Arabian Knights incendiarists in hiding!"

"Small ones, then," said Mr Jones, peering down. "Out you come," he said to Mortimer, who had clambered back in, "and let's have a look. What the blazes *is* all this?"

He dragged out Mortimer, along with various bits of metal.

"It must be one of those medium range conjectures," said Mrs Jones.

The clock struck two.

Then Mr Jones pulled out a sign which said "Kings Cross Station".

"Oh! My lord!" he groaned. "It's Amstring's station. This will be the *end* of us in Rainwater Crescent. Mortimer – how could you *do* it?"

Outside, in Rainwater Crescent, Bill and Joe
were hopping along the street, carrying between
them Mr Coughtrack's bushy kangaroo. As they
hopped they sang:

"Knit for the Islands
Knit for the dry lands
Knit a little bit for Island Aid
We'll win the cruise, we got it made!"

"I'll have to return all this stuff tomorrow," said Mr Jones, gazing despairingly at the tangle of railway-track and bits of stations on the kitchen floor. "I dunno *how* I'm going to apologise –"

"Well, *I* don't see how Mortimer could have fetched all that stuff in," said Mrs Jones. "He wouldn't have had the *time*."

"Then how did he know they were there?"

"'Cos he saw the percolator put them there!"

"Was that it, Mortimer?" asked Arabel.

Mortimer had just taken a sugarlump from the bowl on the table.

"Kssssssrk," he said, his beak full of sugar.

"But why should the son-of-a-brass-monkey want to put the stuff inside *our* clock?"

"Malice," said Mrs Jones. "Or to put the police off the scent. Here, pack all the things in here for now." She had fetched a black garbage sack, and helped her husband fill it with railway. "Arabel, time you went to bed! What about Mortimer?"

"I think he'd like to sleep inside the clock," said Arabel; and kindly helped Mortimer settle in there.

The clock struck three.

Up at the playground Bill and Joe, singing and hiccupping, were trying to cram Mr Coughtrack's bushy kangaroo into the Bottle Bank.

"We'll have to lop the tail off," said Joe. He did so.

"What if they come to empty it?" said Bill.

"The Council? Are you kidding? They won't be doing *anything* till they find their lost room, remember?" He burst into song.

"Mr Mayor lost his room,
 Bill and Joe have found it.
 Now there's not a penny in it,
 Just a tape around it."

"Shut up, you fool!" hissed Bill, aiming a swipe at his colleague.

They fell over in a tangle of arms and legs and kangaroo.

"Ow! my leg!" yelled Joe. "I believe it's broke. Nurse! Nurse!"

6

Next morning Mrs Jones was washing the breakfast dishes, Arabel and Mortimer were buying more wool from the corner shop, and Mr Jones was upstairs shaving, when there came a bang on the front door.

"Who is it?" demanded Mrs Jones, cautiously opening it.

It was the dustman.

"Work-to-rule instructions from the Town Hall," he said. "During the present emergency, only one bag per household. You got two. *And* I gashed me leg on a spike sticking out of one of 'em. Probly get tetanus an' die while the ambulance service is suspended –"

"There's nothing wrong with our rubbish!" retorted Mrs Jones. "This rubbish has been personally inspected by Police Constable Barnoff only last night!"

Now Mr Jones came running downstairs with shaving cream on his face.

"The sock, the *sock*!" he whispered to his wife. "You didn't throw it out, did you?"

"Sock, what sock?"

Mr Jones dived at one of the two black plastic garbage bags.

"Heavens to mercy, he can't have this!"

He displayed the contents to Mrs Jones.

"Oooh, my goodness, why didn't you say?"
she cried. And, to the dustman, "No, no, you
can't have *that* one. No, very sorry."

"Make your mind up!" he snapped, picking
up the other. "Sure you can bear to part with
this?"

"Wait, just a minute," said Mr Jones. He
murmured to his wife, "*Did* you throw away
that sock?"

"*What* sock?"

"That Mortimer had on last night. On his
head."

60

"Of *course* I did! You don't know *whose* it might have been."

"That's just the point! It's evidence that there was a burglar."

Mr Jones rummaged in the dustman's sack, and found the sock, with a milk-top stuck to it.

"No diamond tiaras?" said the dustman sourly, and went clanking off down the road.

Mr Leggit stopped him.

"What did they want? Out of that bag?"

"What's it to you?" said the dustman. "You from MI5 or something?"

"Looking for some stolen property."

"All this fuss about an old sock!" said the dustman. "Anyway your neighbour's got it."

Farther along the street, Mr Jones's other neighbours were in a terrible state about their front gardens.

"Ten years it took, to perfect that kangaroo!" roared Mr Coughtrack.

"My entire re-creation of the three main London railway stations – vanished overnight! My life's work, the comfort of my sunset years, gone!" mourned Mr Amstring.

"And what about my sunflowers?" demanded Mr Leggit, not to be outdone. "Smashed – trampled – when I lay my hands on those idiots – !"

"What idiots? *I* have informed the police,"

said Coughtrack. "They'll soon track down the marauders."

Arabel and Mortimer were returning along the street with their shopping basket just as Mr Jones came out of Number Six with a bulging black sack.

"Nevermore!" said Mortimer ominously, when he saw Mr Leggit.

"I never knew that bird could talk!" said Leggit, much startled.

"He only says *nevermore* when something upsets him," said Arabel.

"Oh – that's all right then. Lovely day, Mr Jones," said Leggit, noticing Mr Jones gazing at his bare feet.

"Oh – er yes," absently agreed Mr Jones, and he went on to where Mr Amstring knelt among the ruins of his stations, and said, awkwardly, "Good morning, Mr Amstring. Er – something most extraordinary has happened – I don't know quite how to explain –"

He held out the black sack.

Mr Amstring stared at him, then began pulling out the contents of the sack.

"St Pancras! Victoria! Kings Cross! *Mangled!* I should have guessed who did it! That bird must be exterminated *immediately!*"

"No, no, Mr Amstring!" interrupted Mr Jones. "The bird's not to blame. It was a plant –"

"Mine was a plant too!" shouted Coughtrack.

"An extremely valuable one – until that walking chainsaw came along –"

"I suppose you instructed your pet to ravage our gardens so you could win the Gala prize by default?" suggested Leggit spitefully.

"Certainly not!" said Mr Jones. "There were burglars in the Crescent last night. We have proof."

At this moment an alarm bell went off inside Mortimer. Mr Jones's watch, in his stomach, played "Twinkle, Twinkle, Little Star".

Even Mortimer looked at bit startled at this. And so did everybody else.

Arabel said, "I think Mortimer's found your watch, Pa."

Mr Jones was frozen with shock, but Amstring exclaimed, "The police have already been informed about this malicious damage, and that bird will be wanted for questioning. I'll see he's locked up for this!"

"Locked up? Mortimer?" gasped Arabel.

"Come on, Arabel, let's go home," said Mr Jones, feeling things were getting out of control. "That's the last time I try to be neighbourly."

Up at the playground, Bill and Joe were drinking beer and eating chips and discussing how they would manage on the cruise, with Joe's broken leg.

"I see myself on crutches, Long John Silver type, green velvet jacket, earrings, might get a parrot –"

"How can you pick pockets in that rig?" said Bill.

The phone rang in the callbox. Bill went slowly to answer it, and listened for some time as a voice barked at him out of the receiver. Then he came back to Joe looking dazed. He said:

"That was Leggy. He wants us to steal a *sock*. From Jones the Taxi. *Now*. In broad daylight!"

Joe gaped at him, quite silenced.

At Number Six, Rainwater Crescent, Mrs Jones was listening to a TV announcement on Network Rumbury.

Grandly dressed in his plumed hat and chain of office, but nonetheless looking decidedly haggard and battered, Mayor Saddlejoy was saying:

"We must apologise for the various delays and cancellations in local services. We are doing out utmost to restore – er – normal life as soon as possible. And a reward of *(gulp)* ten thousand pounds will be paid for the return of the missing

64

tapes; anybody with information should contact
Rumbury Police –"

"Well I never!" murmured Mrs Jones. "Ten
thousand pounds! Just to get our knitting
patterns back. Makes you proud to be a member
of society!"

Then she went back to counting stitches.

At the Town Hall, Doreen said to the Mayor,
"You looked lovely, Your Worship, I was proud
of you. It's wonderful what a dab of mascara
will do."

"Where am I going to get ten thousand
pounds for the reward?" groaned Mr Saddlejoy.

"Well," said Doreen, "if we get the tapes back
we can open the safe-deposit room –"

"But there's nothing *in* the safe! We've been in the red for years. and I'm supposed to judge that blessed Garden Gala tomorrow – let alone count the woolly offerings for Island Aid. Oh, for heaven's sake – *stop knitting!*"

At lunchtime Mr Jones came home to Rainwater Crescent and looked rather glumly at Mortimer, who, now that he was used to having a watch playing tunes inside him, rather enjoyed the sensation. He was twirling round on the table while the watch played "Here We Go Round the Mulberry Bush".

"At least," said Arabel to her father, "you know where it is."

"What use is that? I'm not carrying *him* round with me all day!"

The doorbell rang, and Arabel went to answer it.

Outside in the front garden was Joe, on crutches, wearing a pirate hat, with his leg in plaster.

"Morning, missy!" he said, beaming at Arabel. "Got any old bones? Any rags? Any old irons you don't need, or, indeed, socks? Even just *one* odd sock you don't want?"

"I'll ask," said Arabel, and went back to the kitchen.

Mortimer stayed in the hall, studying Joe's plaster leg.

66

"Hey!" said Joe, struck with an idea. "Here – pretty Polly!"

In the kitchen Mrs Jones was demanding of her husband: "What I want to know is, where did that sock come from? The one that was on Mortimer's head?"

Arabel came back into the room. She said: "There's a pirate outside the front door. He's collecting old socks."

7

"There's a pirate at the front door, asking for old socks," Arabel told her parents.

They stared at each other.

"It must be the burglar, come to revolve the evidence!" whispered Mrs Jones. "Ben! Phone the police!"

"But the phone's in the front hall. He'll hear me."

Meanwhile Joe, helped by Bill, who had followed him pushing a wheelbarrow, was trying to entice Mortimer from the doorway of Number Six. Mortimer was staring hard at the toes sticking out of Joe's plaster leg. Joe was twiddling the toes.

"Here, boy, then! Here, chick, chick, chick, chick!"

Mortimer suddenly made a dive towards the toes.

"Yike!" screamed Joe. "Get him off me!"

He fell backwards into the barrow. Bill, unnerved, started running along the street, pushing the barrow with Joe in it and Mortimer still attached to Joe's toe. They cannoned into Mr Coughtrack, walking home with two heavy bags of shopping.

At this point Mr Jones and Arabel came racing from the open door of Number Six.

"What *happened*?" said Mr Jones, helping Coughtrack to his feet.

By now Bill and Joe, and the barrow, were nearly out of sight.

"Are you all right, Mr Coughtrack?" said Arabel. "Thank you very much for saving Mortimer!"

She stroked Mortimer, who was perched on the fence, putting his feathers straight.

"That was the *last* thing I had in mind!" snarled Coughtrack furiously.

Now Mrs Jones, too, came running out, armed with an aerosol can in each hand.

"Where's the pirate?" she cried.

"Pirate?" said Mr Coughtrack. "The whole Jones family should be *locked up*!"

He took himself indoors with his shopping.

Mr Jones went home and phoned the police.

"Our intruder returned," he said. "I think he was trying to take a hostage. – Yes, I can be at the police station in half an hour. Yes, I'll bring my daughter; she can describe the caller."

"We'll leave Mortimer at home with your Ma," he told Arabel. "At least we know he's a good watchdog."

Mrs Jones put the sock in a paper bag.

"The sooner that's out of this house, the happier I'll be; a garment of ill-omen it is. Don't you worry about your Peter O'Dactyl, my love, he and I'll get along just fine. I'll make an apple pie; that ought to keep him happy."

"And *whose* sock is this?" asked Sergeant Cutlink at the police station.

"Well," said Mr Jones, "somebody last night put it on our bird's head. The burglar who took our cassette player. And then, today, he had a try at kidnapping him."

"Dressed up as a pirate," added Arabel. The Segeant looked confused and doubtful.

"Umn. – Is he available for questioning, this bird? Can he talk?"

"He can say *nevermore*."

"*Very* interesting," remarked the Sergeant. He picked up the sock, rather carefully, on the tip of his Biro, sealed it inside a plastic bag, and put the bag in a drawer.

At Number Six, Rainwater Crescent, Mrs Jones, as promised, was making an apple pie, helped (to some extent) by Mortimer, who was throwing apple peel over his shoulder.

The doorbell rang.

Putting the chain on, Mrs Jones opened the door a crack and peered through.

"RSPCA," said the man outside. "I've had notice of possible malpractice in this household. May I come in?"

"The idea!" said Mrs Jones, outraged. "My Arabel she's a wanted child, I'd have you know. And this is a salutary home!"

"This is about your *pet*, madam. The name mentioned was Mortimer."

"*Mortimer?* We offered him a home out of the goodness of our heart. And he's *perfectly* clean – so far as we can tell –"

"I have information, Mrs Jones, that this pet of yours has swallowed a kangaroo. May I see the bird?"

"No, you may not!" snapped Mrs Jones.

The phone rang.

"You'll have to be excused now, *if* you don't mind," she told the man, and shut the door in his face.

"No, I'm afraid Mr Jones is out," she said sharply to the person on the phone. "Yes, he may have been inspecting your call, but he had to go out imminently on police business. We had an unforeseen intruder last night."

She heard a watery noise from the kitchen.

"Excuse me, I'll have to cut you short. Yes, yes, the minute he gets back –"

In the kitchen Mrs Jones found a flood, caused by Mortimer who had wrapped himself in skeins of wool, turned on both taps, and was happily watching the result from the windowsill. When Mrs Jones made a grab for him, he toppled backwards out of the window, falling, as it chanced, on the RSPCA inspector, who was crouched in the garden, trying to inspect the premises from outside. There was a loud squawk, and a scuffle.

"Ooh!" cried Mrs Jones, looking out. "You stop that, sir! Put that bird down *this minute!*"

She opened the back door, and Mortimer hurtled in, trailing strands of wool behind him.

The inspector followed.

"You have not been invited into our house!" said Mrs Jones indignantly.

But he was just as indignant.

"Now that I see the conditions in which this bird is kept – water everywhere! – tied up in wool – wrongly fed, I daresay – I shall certainly be obliged to check his stomach contents –"

"In my day," cried Mrs Jones, "a householder had rights of entry against this kind of thing –"

"I'm sorry," said the inspector, buckling the astonished Mortimer into a sort of strait-jacket, "but I have information that this bird swallowed a kangaroo, besides some railway stations –"

"That bird consists of an entirely vegan diet! Besides, what he eats is completely on his own head!"

"We'll let you know as soon as we have the results of the autopsy – the medical examination," said the inspector triumphantly, and, carrying Mortimer, he let himself out of the front door.

Up at the children's playground, Bill and Joe had stuck up a sign on the gate which said: DANGER. OUT OF USE. Hidden behind a bush, they were conferring with Mr Leggit.

"Well, you might have *warned* us about the bird," said Joe. "Anyway, don't tell me you only have *one* pair of socks? Bill could pop round to the shops for you?"

"Oh, never mind, never mind," said Leggit crossly. "Now we have to decide where and when to collect the reward money and deliver the tapes. Ten thousand – hm, not bad at all – I didn't think they had that much at the Town Hall to rub together."

"We could say we found it in the kangaroo?" said Bill hopefully."

"Or in that raven?" said Joe.

"So where *is* the tape?" demanded Leggit.

Bill scrabbled in the sandpit and produced three heavy plastic carrier bags.

"What's all that?" said Leggit suspiciously.

"Ah, well, you see," Joe told him, "that was the trouble, there were hundreds at the Town Hall. So we just took them all."

In Rainwater Crescent, Mrs Jones, waving a tea-cosy, was shouting at Mr Coughtrack:

"You are a heartless, soulless man, Mr Coughtrack! How could you *do* such a thing? Inform on our family pet?"

"It's quite simple, Mrs Jones," said Mr Coughtrack, who was angrily sweeping his square of front garden with a brush and dustpan. "You bring back my kangaroo, I withdraw my complaint to the RSPCA."

"But what shall I tell my Arabel?" she wailed. "*We* don't know a blessed thing about your abnegated kangaroo – but you've had her *pet* locked up in a Raven Pound."

Just at this moment Mr Jones and Arabel arrived back in Mr Jones's taxi.

"What's all this, Martha?" said Mr Jones.

"Ma?" said Arabel anxiously. "Where's Mortimer?"

8

In the kitchen of Number Six, Rainwater Crescent, Mrs Jones and Arabel were writing jam labels. But Arabel was very pale and quiet.

Mrs Jones said consolingly, "I'm *sure* your Dad'll fetch back Mortimer, lovey, just as soon as he gets off work. Those inspectors must have checked him over from beak to claw by now. How they could possibly surmise he'd eaten a whole kangaroo – That Mr Coughtrack's the one who wants his head exhuming."

"Praps they'll find Pa's watch," said Arabel.

"Might get it out of him with one of those intravenous magnets," agreed Mrs Jones, nodding.

The telephone rang. It was Mrs Saddlejoy.

"Lil?" said Mrs Jones, settling herself on the stairs with her knitting. "Well! Listen to this! We've been burgled, attacked by pirates, and the neighbours have had Mortimer kidnapped by the RSVP! I've hardly had a single minute to knit – and it's got to be in by tomorrow, hasn't it? What? Wild dogs roaming the town? – Well, I never! Arabel," she called through to the kitchen. "Could you put on the TV News, dearie, see what it says about the wild dogs? All right, then, Lil. This evening will be fine. Oops, there's the News."

Mrs Jones ran back to listen to the TV newsreader, who was saying:

"Hundreds of unclaimed dogs have escaped from the Rumbury Centre for the Protection of Civic Animals, and are roaming the streets. These dogs may be vicious and should not be approached . . . There has been considerable damage to gardens . . . However the Mayor has said that tomorrow's Garden Gala must go ahead as planned . . ."

"Well, I'm blessed!" said Mrs Jones. "Must tell Ben! Maybe we'd still have a chance with ours, if he were to mow the lawn."

At the Town Hall, Doreen answered the phone, rolled her eyes and said to Mr Saddlejoy:

"It's an anonymous call for the Mayor. D'you want to take it?"

The Mayor was just inspecting a sock in a plastic bag, which had been sent up to him by Sergeant Cutlink. He wound the sock round his neck and took the receiver from his secretary.

In the playground callbox Bill said, in a low, threatening voice:

"If you want your tape back, don't tell no one! It's in a kangaroo. Get us ten thousand smackers, by tomorrow, and you can have the tape *and* the kangaroo. I'll be calling you again. This is our secret – between the two of us – or the tape gets mangled – gettit?"

A large dog leapt up snarling outside.

"Get away, get off, scram!" Bill yelled at it, slamming down the phone.

The dog continued to snarl.

In the Town Hall the Mayor said to Doreen, "But where am I to *get* ten thousand pounds? It's hopeless! I give up! I'll just retire – leave – and go away somewhere quiet."

"Why, that's it!" cried Doreen, all excited. "Retire! Don't you remember? The Mayor's retirement fund! The last Mayor disappeared on a Works Outing, the one before jumped into the

Reservoir. Nobody's claimed it for years . . ."

"Mm," said Mr Saddlejoy. "Maybe you have a point. As for *this* –" He looked disgustedly at the sock. "Cutlink must be losing his marbles, if it's his idea of *evidence*. Throw it out!"

At the police station Cutlink was saying to PC Barnoff:

"Go round at once to the RSPCA Civic Animal Centre and bring back a raven by the name of Mortimer. He's said to have eaten a kangaroo."

PC Barnoff glumly surveyed the bandages on his fingers, and started very slowly towards the door.

Then Sergeant Cutlink rang up the Mayor.

"Ah, Your Worship, listen, we've had a very interesting lead – no, not the sock, I fear that was a red herring – ha, ha, ha – no, the RSPCA have been on to us. It seems your tape may have been swallowed by a bird called Mortimer – they have him at the Animal Centre – he's been playing *music* – we shall have to call upon you to identify the tape – he is also said to have swallowed a kangaroo –"

"Kangaroo?" gasped the Mayor at the other end of the line. "But *they* told *me* that a kangaroo had swallowed the tape –"

Then he remembered that he was not supposed to speak, and bit his tongue.

At the Joneses' house, Mrs Jones was still trying to console her daughter. "There, that's forty cosies and twenty-five scarves done. Now I could use some of these ends to make a new pocket for Mortimer if you like. You could give it to him for a peace overture when he comes home."

Arabel smiled a faint, watery smile.

Just then the announcer on the TV screen said: "Here's the latest on the Town Hall burglary. A bird is helping police with their inquiries. His name has not yet been released, but he has black feathers, about two foot, six inches tall, with a sharp beak."

"Oh, Ma!" gasped Arabel. "Is Mortimer in prison?"

Mrs Jones rushed to the phone and called the RSPCA.

"It's downright egregious!" she said. "Handing over *our pet*, a member of our close-knit family group, to the long arm of the law, without so much as a three-minute warning. What kind of a scenario is that? I shall be notifying my MC by the last post. What you *ought* to be doing is catching all those ravening dogs –"

A dog ran past the window, and Mrs Jones rapped on the glass, shouting, "Shoo!"

"It's really just as well those RSVIPs handed him over to the police," she told Arabel. "They've no idea how to treat a creature of Mortimer's calling. At least we *know* PC Barnacle."

"We could make him a pie," said Arabel, after a lot of thought. "With some combs in it. To take to him in prison."

At the Town Hall, Doreen was on the phone to Mrs Saddlejoy. They were talking about the Mayor's outfit for tomorrow's ceremony. Doreen was absently unscrewing one of her earrings.

"Yes, hang it up overnight. And the hat feathers need a bit of a spray –"

PC Barnoff came into the office with a large cardboard box.

"Righty-ho, then, Mrs Saddlejoy, 'bye-bye," said Doreen, and rang off. "Thank you, Constable, very much," she said, giving PC Barnoff a big smile, and she opened the box.

Mortimer, who had been asleep in it, stood up yawning.

"Aaaaah!" screamed Doreen, and she gave PC Barnoff a swipe on the ear. "If *that's* your idea of a *joke*! Where's His Worship's hat, then?"

"Hat?" said Barnoff, puzzled. "This is the raven. Brought round from the Animal Centre for identification. He's supposed to play music."

"Oo, I'm ever so sorry," said Doreen, recovering. "I thought it was His Worship's outfit. My mistake. Er – would he like a toffee?"

She scratched Mortimer under the chin, and he swallowed her earring.

Mr Jones had come home to Rainwater Crescent, and was demanding: "If Mortimer was able to let all those dogs out of the Civic Centre, why couldn't the silly bird escape himself?"

"He's helping the police with their inquiries," said Mrs Jones with some pride. "Here's his new pocket now, lovey, d'you think he'll like it?"

She showed Arabel a knitted pocket.

"Oh, Ma!" said Arabel, very pleased.

The phone rang.

Mr Jones answered. "Oh, is that you, Barnoff? From the Town Hall? Identification of what? There can't be *two* like him, one's enough. Swallowed the Mayor's tape? You mean the one that was stolen from the Town Hall? But he's not been *near* the place. How could he have? Music coming out of him? Oh, my gawd! I know – yes – but, you see it's not what you think. It's that watch of mine. When we thought we'd been burgled. Well, we *had* been burgled, but the watch bit was Mortimer – hallo? Are you still there? Hallo?"

On Doreen's desk in the Town Hall, Mortimer, who had just bitten through the telephone cord, stared at PC Barnoff. Mr Jones's watch inside him was now playing "Twinkle, Twinkle Little Star".

Sergeant Cutlink came through the door with a tuna-fish sandwich wrapped in silver foil.

"Have you started taping?" he said. "Is that the microphone?"

"No, no, it's *him*."

Mortimer's eyes gleamed when he saw the sandwich. He was particularly fond of tuna-fish wrapped in foil. He pounced on it, and flopped speedily through the door. In the passage outside he encountered the Mayor, who had just tried on his robes and feathered hat.

"Doreen, where's my chain?" Mr Saddlejoy was calling. Then he tripped over Mortimer.

"It's in the safe," Doreen called back.

"Stop that bird!" yelled Sergeant Cutlink, rushing out into the passage.

PC Barnoff grabbed the Mayor's hat, thinking it was Mortimer.

By now, the watch inside Mortimer had changed its tune to "Pop Goes the Weasel".

Mortimer, slightly confused by his collision
with Mr Saddlejoy, was staggering about with a
beak full of tuna sandwich and kitchen foil.

The secret door to the safe-deposit room
suddenly shot open and Mortimer walked
through into the room beyond, carrying his
sandwich.

"He's done it, he's *found* it!" shrieked Doreen. "He's *in* there, *look!*"

"Stop the tape! Catch the bird!" shouted Mr Saddlejoy. "Or he may close the door again —"

"Kaaaaark!" said Mortimer, rather stodgily, from the floor of the safe-deposit room.

Sergeant Cutlink dived between everybody's legs to grab the door and prop it open before it could close again.

9

A welcoming group were assembled in Doreen's office in the Town Hall to receive Mr Jones and Arabel when they came to collect Mortimer. PC Barnoff and Sergeant Cutlink were there, as well as the Mayor and Doreen. Mortimer was pecking at a hamburger on Doreen's desk; but he was not really hungry. He seemed delighted to see Arabel, who carefully hung his new knitted pocket round his neck.

Meanwhile Mr Jones was talking to the Mayor and Sergeant Cutlink.

"We must congratulate you, Mr Jones, on your pet's feat! It is remarkable that he knew the exact moment to play that particular tune – we certainly feel that he deserves the reward of ten thousand pounds for returning the stolen computer tape – though how he obtained *that* in the first place –"

"But, excuse me," said Mr Jones, "it *isn't* a tape, it's a watch, my own watch in fact, a musical alarm-watch – I think Mortimer must have swallowed it the night we were burgled –"

"Perhaps," suggested Cutlink, "the burglar was attempting to conceal the stolen tape in your kitchen? – I understand the missing model railway was discovered there – or so we were informed by your neighbour Mr Amstring –"

"Were you indeed?" said Mr Jones indignantly.

"However," Sergeant Cutlink added, "in consideration of the missing watch, it does seem we have to ascertain *what* exactly is producing music inside your bird."

Mr Jones looked a bit anxious.

"Happily," went on Cutlink, "the Rumbury Police have the very latest equipment. The operation can be carried out quite painlessly in the privacy of your home. Now, given the apparent link between the Town Hall burglary and that in Rainwater Crescent, I think I had better take that sock back to Forensic."

"Sock?" said the Mayor. His jaw dropped. "Sock? Ah, excuse me –" He hurried away, calling, "Doreen! Doreen!"

Back in Rainwater Crescent, Mrs Jones was tying yellow ribbons round the bushes in her front garden.

Mr Coughtrack, passing by in the street, said acidly, "Is this a last-ditch attempt to win the Garden Gala?"

Mrs Jones gave him a gracious, forgiving smile.

"Thanks to your *neighbourly interruption*, Mr Coughtrack," she said, "our bird Mortimer is up for an award. Lo, the conjuring hero comes!"

And while Coughtrack gaped at her, utterly

thrown by this news, she turned to welcome her husband, Arabel holding Mortimer, who jumped out of Mr Jones's taxi, and PC Barnoff, who got out of a police van and said to Mr Coughtrack:

"I'm sorry, Sir, you'll have to move along. There's radiographical equipment being removed from this vehicle."

Suddenly the watch inside Mortimer began to play the "Indian Love-Song".

"Oh, blimey!" cried Mr Jones, clapping a hand to his brow. "That'll be Mr Patel at Heathrow airport. What time is it?"

"Four-thirty," said PC Barnoff.

"Every third Saturday, the Bombay flight – sorry, Martha, got to dash. See you later."

Farther down the street, Mr Leggit, returning home with an evening paper, stopped dead as he observed two policemen carrying a large cardboard box into the Jones house.

"What the deuce?" he muttered.

"*Quite*," said Mr Coughtrack sourly from his garden. "Some people have all the luck."

"They won a fitted kitchen?"

"No, radiographic equipment, the PC said."

"Can Bill and Joe have got the tape inside that bird already?" Leggit muttered to himself.

"Pardon?"

"Well, I hope that it makes his feathers fall out," said Leggit hastily, and went into his house.

In the Joneses' kitchen PC Barnoff and his colleague were studying the instructions that came with their equipment.

"*Use swathe indicators to determine size of subject before entering cylinder,*" read Barnoff. "What's that mean?"

"I dunno."

Arabel was giving strings of spaghetti to Mortimer, who was eating some of them and throwing others over his shoulder to see what shapes they formed.

"*Subject, if live, must **not** eat for half an hour before scanning,*" read Barnoff. "Better get him away from that spaghetti."

"But it's his favourite tea!" said Arabel.

Bill and Joe arrived outside Mr Leggit's gate. Bill, wearing a white coat, pushing Joe, reclined in a supermarket trolley with his leg in plaster extended before him. They had a flag, and a collecting tin.

"Help the afflicted of the Island!" chanted Bill, shaking his tin at Mr Leggit, who was trying to prop up some battered sunflowers.

"*I told you two to lie low!*" hissed Mr Leggit. "Not parade the streets making a spectacle! Get out of here, the place is crawling with cops."

"We tried to phone you –" began Bill.

Mr Leggit darted indoors and reappeared with the Joneses' cassette player.

"Here you are, boys!" he said loudly, stuffing
the player into the trolley under Joe. And, in a
furious whisper, "*Get* back to the park and check
out those tapes. I'll see you tonight –"

As Bill and Joe started along the street, a
policeman came running out of the Jones house.
He looked frantic.

"Sorry, boys, it's all I've got," he mumbled, thrusting a five-pound note at them. Bill and Joe looked at each other in amazement. The policeman jumped into the van and drove off.

Loud shrieks and squawks could be heard coming from Number Six.

At the Town Hall, Doreen answered the telephone and called to Sergeant Cutlink: "It's for you! It's PC Barnoff."

Cutlink was out in the corridor, guarding the open safe-deposit room door.

"You come and mind this door, then, while I take the call," he said. "If anyone comes near, jab them with your knitting. Don't let the door swing shut."

"Oo!" said Doreen.

After speaking on the phone, Cutlink came back to Doreen.

"I'll have to leave you in charge for a while," he said. "You take this –" He handed her a small black box. "If anybody comes, press this button. Unless it's one of my officers, of course. One is on his way here now."

"But what *is* it?" said Doreen, gazing nervously at the box.

In the Joneses' kitchen, things were a little chaotic. The floor was covered in thick, snaking cables. The table was surrounded by screens. Mortimer was lying on the table with a flap over him and his feet sticking out. Mrs Jones was pasting transparent jelly over his throat with a fish slice.

Luckily Mortimer was quite enjoying this.

"Shouldn't he take his pocket off?" Mrs Jones asked. "Before the next bit?"

"Now, if we could borrow your TV?" said PC Barnoff, wheeling in a kind of hood behind Mortimer.

"What ever for?"

Mortimer hurled himself inside the hood.

In their gardens, Mr Amstring and Mr Coughtrack were grumbling.

"Us innocent citizens make a complaint, it's totally ignored," said Coughtrack. "Look at *that*!" as Sergeant Cutlink's car arrived with sirens blaring. "These Joneses and their pestilential pet get royal treatment. But where's my kangaroo? Tell me that?"

In the Town Hall, the Mayor, who had been out to buy sandwiches, returned to find Doreen guarding the safe-deposit door, clutching the black box with both hands.

"What's going on?" he demanded, suddenly coming up behind her.

Doreen fainted dead away.

"Good lord!" muttered the mayor, staring at the box. "It must be a bomb! – Watch out!" he cried to PC Brown, who had just arrived. "It's a *bomb*!"

In the Joneses' kitchen Sergeant Cutlink was saying to Mrs Jones:

"We overlooked this. You have to sign the indemnity form, ma'am."

Using the fish slice, PC Barnoff was trying to get Mortimer out of the hood. The fish slice was tangled in the strings of Mortimer's pocket.

"Oo, I don't know if I *should* sign," said Mrs

Jones doubtfully to Sergeant Cutlink. "I think I'll wait till my hubby gets back. There's nothing to pay, is there?"

Mortimer suddenly shot out of the hood very fast, and clung to Arabel.

PC Barnoff snatched up the kitchen scissors to cut the pocket strings. Mrs Jones, seeing the scissors and thinking Mortimer was about to be stabbed or cut in half, screamed loudly.

The front doorbell rang. It was Mr Coughtrack, who marched right into the house, proclaiming: "This is a citizen's arrest!"

At that moment the telephone rang.

"999! Ambulance!" Mrs Jones shouted into it. Then she listened to what it was saying.

"I want that bird opened up!" roared Mr Coughtrack, bursting into the kitchen and colliding with PC Barnoff. "*He's got my kangaroo!*"

There was a scuffle.

"It's a bomb! At the Town Hall!" shrieked Mrs Jones from the stairs. "They've blown up the Mayor!"

"*What?*" cried Sergeant Cutlink.

Mortimer seized the chance, in all this confusion, to exit through his raven-flap.

"Mortimer, where are you going?" called Arabel.

She opened the back door and ran after him.

10

At the Jones house, PC Barnoff was arresting
Mr Coughtrack for illegal entry and assault on a
police officer. Mrs Jones was weeping for her
lost daughter and raven. Sergeant Cutlink was
on the point of leaving for the Town Hall.

"Got to check out this bomb," he said.
"Seems like it's a hoax; but you never can tell.
You take that man down to the station, Barnoff.
Insulting words and behaviour. It was your own
fault," he said to Coughtrack, who growled at
him. "And report the girl and the bird missing."

Just then Mr Jones came home.

"Oh, Ben!" cried Mrs Jones, rushing to her
husband, "They've gone! Arabel's gone!"

"What's been going *on* here?" demanded
Mr Jones.

Arabel and Mortimer were up at the
playground. Mortimer had ignored the
DANGER sign. Arabel was rocking Mortimer
on the roundabout. Mortimer was hiccupping.

"But you *shouldn't* have bitten that policeman,
you know," she told him. "And I think we'd
better start for home now. It's getting late."

"*Hic!*" said Mortimer. He had swallowed a
great deal of transparent jelly, as well as several
pieces of equipment.

Suddenly he turned his head towards the Wendy-house, listening.

"What *is* it?" whispered Arabel. "Is somebody in there?"

Faint chittering, squeaking sounds came from the Wendy-house, as if it had been occupied by chipmunks.

"Mortimer, let's go!" whispered Arabel nervously.

"Kaaa-*hic*-aark," said Mortimer. He had no intention at all of going just yet.

Sergeant Cutlink arrived at the Town Hall and found Doreen still in a dead faint outside the safe-deposit room door, and PC Brown crawling towards her on his stomach, to reach for the black box.

"Oh, for heaven's *sake*!" said Cutlink crossly. "That's my *radio*, you fool!"

He snatched it up. "Come on, miss," he said to Doreen. "Up you get! You seem to have done a good job here, frightened off the entire Rumbury Force; or *this* ninny, at least."

He switched on his radio and barked orders into it.

"Calling all cars, Sergeant Cutlink speaking. Alert all cars: missing, one small girl, one large raven; little girl named Arabel Jones, last seen in Rainwater Crescent –"

"Ooo!" said Doreen.

At Number Six, Rainwater Crescent, Mr Jones had agreed to take PC Barnoff and Mr Coughtrack, shackled together by handcuffs, to the police station in his taxi. Then he was going on to search for Arabel and Mortimer.

Mrs Jones would remain at home, in case the lost pair came back.

In the Wendy-house at the playground, Bill, Joe and Mr Leggit were playing tape after tape at high speed on Mr Jones's cassette player.

"Why did you have to steal so *many*?" grumbled Leggit. "Can't you tell a computer tape from a Women's Guild Homecrafts Course?"

"It was the gas," said Joe. "I was disguised as an exterminator, see, come to kill the 'roaches. We just grabbed every tape in the building."

"And *why did you have to steal that kangaroo*?"

"That was for *you*, Guv – give you a better chance in the Garden Gala –"

Suddenly a loud voice boomed out from the player.

"*MIND – THE – GAP!*"

"Blimey!" gasped Bill. "What's *that*?"

Outside, in the playground, Arabel, all excited, whispered, "Listen, *listen*, Mortimer, that's Pa's taxi tape!"

97

"Krrrrr – *hic!*" said Mortimer, much interested. Then he began to climb up the roof of the Wendy-house.

"Mortimer, *no!*" whispered Arabel, terrified. "*Please* let's go home!"

At Number Six, Rainwater Crescent, the doorbell rang, making Mrs Jones, who had been about to phone her sister, jump uncontrollably.

She dropped the phone and left it dangling.

The person at the door was Mrs Saddlejoy, come to keep Martha company with her knitting.

"Gracious me, Martha," said Lil. "What ever's been going on here, then?"

Mrs Jones had been too dejected to tidy the kitchen. But now she cheered up just a little.

"I'll make us a nice cup of tea," she said.

The telephone receiver was still dangling.

Up at the playground Arabel watched in horror as Mortimer plunged straight down the chimney of the Wendy-house. At once a terrific racket broke out inside.

Bill came staggering out, and ran off.

"Bill, Bill, *wait!*" implored Joe, crawling out on all fours. "Don't forget *me*, I'm your *pal!*"

He grabbed a stick and began hopping after Bill.

Mr Leggit shot out then, very angry and somewhat damaged, with his trouser leg badly torn.

"Come back!" he shouted furiously. "You'll be sorry! – I won't pay you a penny! Ouch – help – that bird's demented –"

"Mr Leggit!" said Arabel, very astonished.

Mr Jones had stopped at the Town Hall, in case Arabel and Mortimer had gone there. But they had not. Sergeant Cutlink was there, however, and kindly checked on his radio. But there was still no report of the lost pair.

"I'd best give my wife a call," said Mr Jones gloomily.

"My Lil's spending the evening with her," the Mayor told him.

"Oh, that's good." Mr Jones cheered up a little. "Martha's always best in company."

But when he tried his own number, it seemed to be out of order.

After half an hour of knitting and two cups of tea, Mrs Jones said to Mrs Saddlejoy:

"Lil, I can't stand it any longer. The suspense is distraining me. I'm going out to look for them. I'll leave a message on the board, and the back door unlocked –"

"And I'll come with you," said Lil with enthusiasm. "*We*'ll soon find them!"

Out they went, leaving the phone still dangling from the end of its cord.

"I'll go down to your house, Mr Jones," said the Mayor. "I was going to pick up Lil, anyway."

"Oh, would you?" said Mr Jones, pleased. "Then I can go and have a look round the shopping precinct. Mortimer likes the Amusement Arcade."

The two men walked out of the Town Hall together, leaving Sergeant Cutlink still in charge of the open safe-deposit door.

In the Wendy-house at the playground, Arabel was saying to Mortimer:

"*Look*, Mortimer! It's Ma's cassette player! I wonder who all these other tapes belong to?"

Mortimer was not listening.

He had found a very dirty and ragged something, and was crooning and hiccupping over it with unbounded joy.

"Why – my goodness!" said Arabel. "It's your very first pocket. All right, I'll help you put it on; but when we get home we must wash it. It's ever so dirty. I think we'd better take all these tapes too. But they are dreadfully heavy."

Arabel looked and sounded very tired. It had been a long day.

Outside the Wendy-house, Mortimer made a beeline for the Bottle Bank.

"What is it *now*, Mortimer?"

Mortimer, on the rim of the Bottle Bank, began to rummage wildly inside.

Mr Saddlejoy the Mayor was ringing the
doorbell at Number Six, Rainwater Crescent.
But nobody was answering the door.

"That's funny!" muttered Mr Saddlejoy.
"Lil definitely said she was coming here."

A stray dog raced by, barking.

Next door, in his front garden, Mr Leggit
peered angrily through his sunflowers at the
Mayor, who finally sighed, got back into his
car, and drove away.

He went up to the shopping precinct.

There, he found Mr Jones, indignantly saying
to the two ladies, his wife and Mrs Saddlejoy:

"You should have stayed in the Crescent!
Suppose they come home? And find the house
empty?"

"Well, you see, Ben –"

Mrs Saddlejoy quickly said that her feet were
killing her, and she needed a coffee at the Cappo
Chino. Mr Jones was not pleased, but felt he had
to be polite to the Mayor's wife. So he bought
them a coffee.

Up at the playground, Mortimer had managed
to drag Mr Coughtrack's kangaroo out of the
Bottle Bank.

"But we can't take that great thing home,
Mortimer!" said Arabel. Then she recognised it.
"Oh, my goodness! Perhaps we'd better."

Luckily, behind the Wendy-house, she found

the supermarket trolley that Bill had used to
wheel Joe.

"This will be just right," she said, greatly
relieved, and she piled kangaroo, tapes, cassette
player, and, finally, Mortimer, into the trolley.

Just the same, it was a long walk home.

Back at the house in Rainwater Crescent, they
went in by the kitchen door, which was not
locked. Arabel was rather surprised to find no
one at home.

But there was a message on the slate saying "G.T.B. E.S. T.O.G."

"Gone to Bingo?" said Arabel. "E.S. *might* mean Eat Syrup. You can have it, Mortimer. I'm not hungry." In fact, Arabel felt rather sick.

"We'd better put these things away," she said. "In the clock, perhaps."

Mortimer helped her do this.

Arabel left a message on the board. She drew a girl in bed, looking sick. She also made a picture of the clock, with a big X across its front.

Then she went to bed.

Mortimer tipped over the big tin of syrup so that its lid came off. Then he had a lot of the syrup; as much as he could eat. The rest poured down over Mrs Jones's pile of completed knitting, which was on top of the laundry basket.

Then Mortimer made himself a nice gooey, sticky nest in the middle of the pile of knitting, and he, too, went to sleep.

Much later in the evening, Mr and Mrs Jones came home.

11

Next morning Mr Jones, about to go off and drive some children to school, came to ask Arabel if there was anything she would like.

Arabel was feeling very poorly with a sore throat. She was lying on the sofa, wrapped in a quilt, with a thermometer in her mouth, so she could not talk. She drew a big K, for kangaroo, with her finger on the quilt.

"Crayons?" said Mr Jones, puzzled. "I'll get you some, dearie." Then he tiptoed away, leaving Arabel looking slightly frantic. In his worry about Arabel, Mr Jones left his house-keys on the kitchen table.

Mortimer was in a bad temper, because Mrs Jones had hustled him off the sofa, and washed his black-and-white pocket. He was waiting for a chance to go and get the wet pocket off the line.

Meanwhile, as Mrs Jones looked at the thermometer, he began removing things from the clock.

"Oo, my goodness!" said Mrs Jones, staring at the thermometer. "I wonder if we ought to get the doctor. But it's the weekend . . . oh dear . . ."

Absently she picked up her husband's keys and put them in her pocket.

Arabel really only wanted to go to sleep, so Mrs Jones sang her a lullaby:

"Hush, my girlie, don't say a word,
   Pa's gone and got you a big black bird,
   Even if that bird won't sing
   He can eat a diamond ring . . ."

Bill and Joe had returned to the Wendy-house. What they found there – or rather, did not find – threw them into a frenzy.

"They're all *gone* – the tapes and the player – even the blessed kangaroo –"

"I told you that bird was trouble."

"He can't have done it."

"He could do anything."

"We'd better phone Leggy."

Mr Jones, coming home with a newspaper and a shopping bag, saw Mr Leggit limping ahead.

"Morning, Leggit, what happened?" said Mr Jones. "Fall off a ladder, did you?"

"The town's not safe," growled Leggit. "Mongrels everywhere."

Mr Jones went into his own house. He did not notice Mortimer in the front garden, busy pushing objects under the fence. Hearing a loud shriek from the kitchen, Mr Jones hurried through the hall.

"*Look* what's here!" gasped Mrs Jones,

pointing to a large tangled mass of leaves and mess lying in the middle of the floor. "What in the world *is* it? And where did it come from?"

"I can tell you what it is," said Mr Jones gloomily, turning it over, "It's Coughtrack's kangaroo."

He sat down on a chair, looking very tired.

"Poultryghosts!" cried Mrs Jones. "That's what Arabel was trying to tell us. With her picture! That clock is haunted by a collecto-maniac. *That*'s why she did that drawing."

Mr Jones said, "The only kleptomaniac in this house is that bird."

"Well, we'd better get rid of it," said Mrs Jones.

"The bird?"

"No. That kangaroo. We don't want the inspectors coming back, saying we need a licence for it."

Mr Jones, about to put on the kettle for a cheering cup of tea, was stopped dead by seeing the stolen cassette player back on the work-top.

"Arabel must have found it last night," he said.

"Look, Ben, there's a tape in it! Maybe it's the Mayor's tape."

Mr Jones switched on the player.

A distant, booming voice commanded: "*ALL CHANGE. ALL CHANGE! This is the end of the line.*"

"Oo, it's a warning," cried Mrs Jones distractedly.

"No it's not, it's my own taxi tape. – Well, at least that's one good thing."

With some difficulty, Mr Jones picked up the kangaroo, carried it through the front hall, and out through the front door. With his arms full of bush, he failed to see Mortimer, who nipped past him through the open door, carrying a sunflower in his beak. His pocket was trailing on the ground behind him.

Up at the Town Hall, Doreen and PC Brown arrived together, fresh and cheerful. They found Sergeant Cutlink fast asleep in the doorway of the safe-deposit room. Doreen kindly brought the sergeant a paper cup of coffee.

"They've found the little girl," she told him.

"I know *that*," snapped Cutlink. "I've got a radio, haven't I?"

He drank the coffee, which was only luke-warm. Then, leaving PC Brown in charge of the door, he went off to the police station.

At the Jones house, Mrs Jones was washing all her tea-cosies, which were soaked in syrup.

"Oh, well," she sighed, "there's a good wind, they should dry in time for the collection."

She listened to an announcement on the radio:

"The safe-deposit room is still under armed-guard, day and night. Despite the Mayor's offer of a ten thousand pound reward, there is still no sign of the missing computer tape which operates the automatic door. The public are urged to report anything suspicious. The Mayor will be leading the procession to judge the Garden Gala this afternoon . . ."

Mr Jones came back from returning the kangaroo.

"You'd think he'd be *grateful*. But not a bit. The only reason he didn't go to the police is that he's been at the station all night."

"Oh, Ben, could you cut the grass? Just so's the garden's a bit tidy for the Gala Fly-past?"

Mr Jones mowed the small front patch, and Mrs Jones, running out of clothes-line space, perched her tea-cosies on garden stakes all around the flowerbeds.

Then she went indoors, murmuring, "Arabel'll be waking soon, I'd better get the lunch started. Maybe a nice roast leg —"

Mortimer, who was inside the clock, heard this and came hopefully hopping out, bringing with him a mass of sunflowers.

"*Help!*" shrieked Mrs Jones, dropping the joint of mutton. "Help, help, Ben, it's the polluterghost!"

Leaving the fridge door open, she rushed out of the kitchen, through the hall, and out through the front door.

At Rumbury police station, PC Barnoff was saying to Sergeant Cutlink:

"I don't think we've heard the last of that Coughtrack and his kangaroo, sir. He *still* insists the bird's responsible."

"It isn't impossible," said Cutlink. "Hmn. I think what we might do there is kill two birds with one stone."

"*Sir?*"

"Get me Rumbury Hospital," said the sergeant.

At Number Six, Rainwater Crescent, Mr and Mrs Jones had got themselves locked out of the house. She had run screaming out of the front door, slamming it behind her. And Mr Jones had left his keys indoors.

The back door was bolted.

"You told me last night always to leave it bolted," sobbed Mrs Jones.

Mr Jones peered through the kitchen window. He saw a bottle of milk topple out of the open refrigerator door.

"There! See! It *is* haunted," wept Mrs Jones. "It's the portholeghost. We'll have to get the church to expropriate it. I should have bought that garlic from the bicycle salesman. Now I can hear the phone ringing! And Arabel's all alone in the house."

"No, she's not, Mortimer's with her," said Mr Jones grimly, seeing Mortimer emerge from the fridge with a rasher of bacon in his beak.

At the police station PC Barnoff said: "The
Joneses aren't answering, Sergeant. – Oh, just a
minute. Somebody's saying Kaaaark. Must be
an Ansafone?"

"Leave a message then," Cutlink said crossly.

"Hallo. Hallo. This is Rumbury police
station," said PC Barnoff.

Arabel, woken by the phone, came sleepily into
the front hall. She felt a little better. She saw
Mortimer peering into the receiver, which lay
on the stairs. Out of it came a voice, which said:

"We have to perform a painless operation on
your raven in order to ascertain the definite
whereabouts of the Mayor's tape; also missing
kangaroo. Please contact us without delay –"

Arabel, terribly shocked, wrapped her arms
round Mortimer. She could not speak, her
throat was too sore.

12

Just as the fire brigade arrived, Mrs Jones remembered that she had picked up Ben's keys off the kitchen table and put them in her apron pocket. She opened the front door of Number Six, Rainwater Crescent, and rushed inside, calling, "Mum's just coming, dearie!"

"Very sorry for your trouble," Mr Jones told the firemen.

"OK, chaps, false alarm!" called the fire chief to his men, who were all piling out of the truck with axes and ladders.

"False alarm it is *not*!" exclaimed Mrs Jones, reappearing indignantly in the front doorway. "There's a spook in our clock and it has terrorised our child. She's in a dreadful state!"

"Spooks ain't our department," said the fire chief. "We'll be off – got to play in the Brass Band this afternoon – Mayor's procession."

They roared away, under the angry stares of Mr Coughtrack, Mr Amstring and Mr Leggit.

Mrs Jones had run back indoors, and was hugging Arabel, who, with tears pouring down her cheeks, could say nothing, but only point speechlessly at Mortimer.

The telephone still hung at the end of its cord. But it was silent now. Mr Jones thoughtfully put the receiver back on its rest.

At the far end of the street Bill and Joe, who had acquired a pile of evening papers from somewhere, were shouting:

"All the latest! Read all about it! Disclosures! Garden Gala imbroglio!"

They even managed to sell a paper to Mr Amstring.

At Number Six, Arabel's parents were hovering about her anxiously.

"Was it Mortimer who pinched Mr Leggit's flowers?"

Arabel gave a sad nod. She still could not speak.

"*And* Mr Coughtrack's kangaroo?"

She shook her head.

"Well, don't you worry, lovey, your Pa'll manage to sort it all out. You get back on the sofa all wrapped up warm. *You*," Mrs Jones told her husband, "had best pop out and get a lemon and some honey. *And* some sausages and milk – don't fancy that joint after it's had sunflowers and kangaroos dragged all over it on the floor –"

"All right," said Mr Jones. "Here's the drawing book and crayons I got you earlier, Arabel, dearie."

She perked up just a little, and, as he went out, opened the book and began to draw.

Bill and Joe, having worked their way with newspapers all along the street, were hiding among the sunflowers in Leggit's front garden. They watched Mr Jones as he got into his taxi and drove away.

Mrs Jones, without observing Bill and Joe, came out and dropped an armful of sunflowers over the fence on top of them.

"Oh, my hay-fever," mumbled Bill, sneezing, as Mrs Jones went back indoors.

Mr Leggit heard the noise and came out.

"*What are you doing to my sunflowers?*" he said. "Idiots – nincompoops – peabrains – !"

"Here, what the blazes are all these?" mumbled Joe, finding tapes among the sunflower stalks.

"It's the tapes!" cried Bill. "D'you mean, Leggy, you had 'em all along?"

"Had what?" snarled Leggit. Then, he, too, saw the tapes.

"*Why* did you bring those *here*?"

"We didn't – it must have been that flaming bird!"

"Well, *get rid of them* – chuck them over the fence! Any time now, the Mayor will be along – if these are seen here we're in the soup –"

Mr Amstring came out into his garden.

"Afternoon, Leggit! What's happened to your flowers? Looks like a goat's broken loose from the Civic Centre."

"Ah, just a little accident," said Leggit hastily. "These boys are here to fix it."

"Ask me, there's foul play afoot," said Amstring gloomily.

"Fowl play! Ha, ha! Very good!" agreed Leggit, wishing his neighbour would go indoors.

Mrs Jones was bringing Arabel a big pan full of hot water and mustard.

"Here, lovey, just pop your feet in there. But take your slippers off first."

Arabel showed her mother a picture she had drawn of Mortimer strapped on an operating table, and a man in a white coat with a knife in his hand.

"Good gracious me, what's that, Mortimer in hospital? No, no, *you*'re the one that's sick. Not him. Now you sit there nice and warm, and I'll just hang this last lot of cosies out to dry."

116

Off went Mrs Jones. Arabel rather hopelessly laid down her book, got up, and went to the back door, leaving a trail of wet, mustardy footprints.

The phone rang.

Mrs Jones came running in to answer it.

"*What?*" she exclaimed. "Police? You should be ashamed of yourselves, browbeating an innocent child, left all alone in the house with a paltryghost! Take Mortimer to hospital? Mr Jones would not *hear* of such a thing." She slammed down the receiver.

Then she phoned Doreen at the Town Hall.

"Complain to the Mayor?" said Doreen. "But, Mrs Jones – I'm afraid he's just gone off, in the procession, you know. I'll tell him later."

Crossly, Mrs Jones hung up. Then the doorbell rang. It was Mr Coughtrack.

"And to what do we owe the horror of this visit?" said Mrs Jones acidly.

Mr Coughtrack said: "I've come to demand a full apology and confession of your bird's misdeeds in front of the Mayor, who is –"

Mrs Jones said, "Mayor? You'll have to speak to the Bishop. Our Mortimer has been overtaken by a pantryghost."

"You mean he's possessed?" gasped Mr Coughtrack.

"Well – actually he's the property of my daughter, but I speak for her –"

Just at this moment PC Barnoff arrived, to

pick up the radiograph equipment.

"Now, then, sir!" he said to Mr Coughtrack, "you were warned once before about harassing your neighbours."

"I'm not staying here!" shouted Coughtrack. "They're all deranged."

Arabel had found Mortimer in the back garden, had managed to smuggle him into the house, buttoned inside her dressing gown, and had hidden him in what she thought would be a safe place.

Now she was horrified to see PC Barnoff come into the hall with Mrs Jones, and pick up the large cardboard carton of assorted radiographic equipment.

But luckily, as Barnoff walked down the front path with it, Mortimer burst out of the top and flapped away, scattering pieces of polystyrene packing. He dived under the fence and into Leggit's garden.

At this moment the sound of a brass band came joyfully from the end of the street.

Outside Mr Coughtrack's garden the Mayor, Mr Saddlejoy, in his robes and feathered hat, and his wife Lil, in her fur coat and bouquet, were looking rather doubtfully at the topiary kangaroo.

It had been bandaged, and propped up in a deckchair with a sign in front that said: SABOTAGED BY POLTERGEIST.

"Is that the name of the species?" cautiously asked Lil.

"It's that *raven* that did it," growled Mr Coughtrack.

"Oh? How clever," said the Mayor politely. "How clever of him."

Mortimer, who had been overjoyed to find his pocket, which he had dropped among Mr Leggit's sunflowers, was returning home with it when he met PC Barnoff, come back for another load of equipment.

"Here, birdie. Birdie?" said PC Barnoff hopefully.

In the next-door garden Mr Leggit had come out with a large butterfly-net.

"See if you can catch the bird with this," he told Bill and Joe. "And *get rid of* those tapes over the fence –"

"Can't, there's a cop in there," said Bill. "And here comes Jones in his taxi."

Mr Jones hurried up his front path, carrying two bags of groceries. Doreen was with him.

"So glad I met you," she was saying. "Your wife's in such a state as never was about that poor bird –"

Sergeant Cutlink jumped out of a police car, and Doreen turned on him.

"You should be ashamed. You can't let them do it!" Doreen shouted at him.

"Do what?" said Cutlink.

Arabel was at the front window. She waved frantically to Mortimer, and banged on the glass to attract his attention and persuade him to come inside. Mortimer saw her, but dived back to Mr Leggit's side of the fence.

By now the Mayor and his party had moved on to Mr Amstring's garden, where the stations and bits of railway-track had been rather hastily pieced together.

"Looks as if there's been a bit of an earthquake here?" said Mr Saddlejoy.

"*I* believe the Joneses' bird was at the bottom of it," said Mr Amstring sourly.

Mrs Saddlejoy tactfully interrupted: "I wonder what is going on in the next garden?"

All hell seemed to have broken loose among Mr Leggit's sunflowers. There were shouts, screams and crashes.

Arabel, still watching through the window, could bear it no longer, and dragged Mrs Jones out into the front garden of Number Six.

"All right, all right," cried Mrs Jones, cramming a tea-cosy on her daughter's head and one on her own, "but if you catch your death, don't tell *me* about it –"

Mortimer appeared triumphantly on the fence between the Leggit and Jones gardens. He had his pocket dangling round his neck, and a white cassette in his beak, from which yards of tape streamed behind him in the wind.

Arabel ran towards him. "*Mortimer!*" she cried.

"Oh my goodness gracious!" said Mrs Jones.

Sergeant Cutlink and PC Barnoff, who had been talking to Mr Jones, turned at all the commotion, and saw Bill and Joe in Leggit's garden.

"Why," said Barnoff, "it's the Cash and Carry Boys. What the blazes are they doing here?"

"*Come* on, Barnoff!" roared the sergeant, racing along the street. "Grab them!"

And they grabbed the two boys.

Meanwhile Arabel was carefully lifting Mortimer off the fence.

"This is intolerable!" snapped Mr Leggit, who had also been seized by the police. "What grounds have you for this outrageous behaviour?"

"Concealing stolen goods on your premises. Consorting with known malefactors," said Cutlink, snapping the handcuffs on him.

"I wish to phone my lawyer!"

"You can do it from the station," said Barnoff, bundling him into the police van.

"Cutlink, what is all this?" inquired the Mayor. "Are those the tapes from the Town Hall?"

"Maybe, sir," said Cutlink, gazing at all the strands of tape blowing about among the sunflowers. "But whether they are any *use* now —"

Doreen screamed, "*Ooooo!*"

She was pointing at Mortimer, who was twirling round and round on the Joneses' birdbath, still with the white cassette in his beak, and Arabel, who was following him, trying to gather up the tape as it came unwound.

"That's the one!" cried Doreen, her eyes sparkling. "For the safe-deposit room door. That clever bird has found it!"

"Well I'm blessed," said Mr Jones.

Lil Saddlejoy, following her husband, gazed into the Joneses' garden.

"Gracious, Martha! You sly thing! What a nobby idea!" she said, looking at all the brilliant tea-cosies on stakes. "Do look, dear!" she called to her husband. "But, just fancy, Martha, your living next-door to those hardened criminals all this time —"

"Mmmm. Very decorative," murmured the
Mayor, looking over the fence.

"These?" said Mrs Jones, embarrassed. "Why,
they are just my little offering for the
disembodied of Pollyargy."

"Philanthropic, too," said Mr Saddlejoy.
"A charming idea."

He consulted with his wife, then said:

"Mr and Mrs Jones, I am delighted to present
you with the first prize in the Rumbury Garden
Gala – a cruise for all your family to the island of
Polyandros."

Arabel, who had now managed to get the
cassette away from Mortimer, politely handed it
to Mr Saddlejoy.

"*And* the reward of ten thousand pounds," suggested Sergeant Cutlink, giving the Mayor a nudge, "for return of the stolen tape."

"Ah indeed, yes, yes, of course," said the Mayor hastily, "the reward, the reward for your clever pet."

"He's not a pet, he's a poltergeist," shouted Mr Coughtrack furiously over the fence.

"They sabotaged our gardens in order to win," chimed in Mr Amstring.

"Now, gentlemen, gentlemen, come, come! Is this the spirit of sporting losers? Besides, there will be second prizes –"

But, since the neighbours continued to grumble and fume, the sergeant told them:

"It'll all come out at the trial, you'll see. I reckon that Leggit was behind it all. I've had my eye on him for some time."

"Trying to put the blame on a poor dumb bird!" said Mrs Jones.

"NEVERMORE!" shouted Mortimer, and, becoming rather dizzy, he toppled off the bird-bath, playing "Yankee Doodle".

Arabel ran to catch him.